BIG MAN

USA TODAY Bestselling Author
PENNY WYLDER

ISBN-13: 978-1979413350
ISBN-10: 1979413355

Chapter 1

Sasha Bluebell

The letter arrives at the worst possible time.

I'm currently between clients, juggling freelance jobs from my last company, where I was their head paralegal consultant until I had enough of their bullshit pseudo-assignments and quit to pursue my own thing.

But it's been slow-going in the freelance world, and it's taken me a while to build up a private client base. Originally I took on a couple of gigs for my old firm on a case-by-case basis. Now they've flooded me with so many that it feels like I'm full-time again, minus the healthcare benefits.

Not that I can complain about the money. That, at least, has been more than decent.

Still, my schedule is a wreck. So much a wreck, that when the letter first arrives, I don't even notice it in my inbox for a week straight. When I do, I take one glance at the cover letter and find myself wincing, wanting to shove it straight back under the stack of unread incoming mail that awaits me on my desk. The longer I can prolong this, the better. Because I don't want to confront any of the emotions that rise up when I read that first line.

In the Matter of the Estate of Maryanne Bluebell...

No, thank you. I spent a year after Mama died being heartbroken. I don't need to relive that again, thank you very much. Besides, it took her estate that whole year and an extra 8 months to even get this letter to me. How important could it be?

But eventually, after a week of ignoring that half-opened letter on my desk while I sorted through my current freelance projects, I ran out of excuses. I couldn't prolong the inevitable anymore. I had to face the music.

I unfolded the full letter over a hefty pour of Cabernet one Friday night, with my favorite cheesy TV reality show on in the background, and a long-overdue weekend off ahead of me. I figured that might mitigate the blow, knowing that for once I had some free time to myself coming up. I'd worked overtime for the last month and a half straight to carve myself this little slice of freedom.

And this is how I decided to reward myself? I really am a masochist in disguise.

By the time I reach the third line of the letter, I've already downed my whole glass of Cab. I need to refill to finish reading. Because this one, I didn't see coming.

I didn't expect the middle block of text, written by my mother herself, years before her death.

I didn't expect the plea to resonate so deeply.

I didn't expect to feel it in my bones when I read her words on the page, ink long-dried, words she asked her lawyer to add to this case file long before the breast cancer stole her from me.

Sasha,

You are my only legacy. I don't say this because I'm ashamed of it—you are the best thing that ever happened to me. My dearest dream in life was to raise you right, and I am so proud of the woman you have become.

I know how much you love your life in the city, and I'm happy that you've found your place. But I hope you recognize the history and importance of our home back here, too. Your great-great grandfather built this house with his own hands. For generations, your family has tilled the soil, lived off what this land produced. I hope that when I am gone, you will respect the legacy we've both been entrusted with and do what is right for this place.

If you're reading this letter, it all belongs to you now, my love. I trust you with it, as I trust you with everything in my life.

Your loving mother

She left it unsigned. That, somehow, makes it sting even worse.

I just keep rereading the words *this place* and *our home*. She means the family farm back in Nowheresville. That place and I haven't been on speaking terms for fifteen years. Not since I applied to the farthest college away that would take me, packed up my bags and got the fuck out of dodge.

I've spent the last fifteen years right here in New York City. I can't imagine going back. Hell, I barely even *visited*, not until two years ago, right at the end, when things were so bad Mama couldn't make it on a plane out here. She visited me in the city as often as she liked because I couldn't stand to visit her.

I visited that one time. The last time. I held her hand as she closed her eyes and breathed her last. I barely stayed long enough to sign the estate over to my more-than-capable legal team and then I high-tailed it out of dodge.

I never thought I'd need to go back. I never planned to set foot in that tiny town ever again.

But here are her words, staring up at me in

black-and-white, asking the impossible. Asking me to return.

I can't, is my immediate gut reaction.

You have to, is what my frontal cortex yells at my monkey brain.

Because how can I ignore this letter? How can I disregard the last wishes of my mother when I'm her only child, her only heir, the only one she ever had to lay all her hopes and dreams on?

I fold the letter back up, for tonight. For tonight, I concentrate on my shitty reality TV show and my bottle of Cabernet, which I'm definitely going to polish off by myself, propriety be damned.

For tonight, I let myself enjoy the first day off I'd managed to carve in my schedule since as long as I can remember. Life here in the city is hectic, but it's what I love. There's always something going on, always a new project to focus on, always something to occupy my attention. Much better than country life. Much better than that stifling hometown I escaped the first minute I could.

For tonight, I enjoy the life I built myself, on my own sweat and blood and tears and exhaustion.

Then the next morning, hung-over and bleary-eyed from lack of sleep, I unfold the letter one more time and dial the number at the bottom.

"Paul?" I ask the moment the estate handler picks up. "I need to book a flight back home…"

And that's how the real trouble began.

Chapter 2

Sasha Bluebell

This is going to be a tactical strike, I tell myself as I stomp on the gas of my rental car. It took me three hours—*three hours*—to drive here from the regional airport. And that was after two connecting flights, because somehow, this Podunk town doesn't even have a single direct flight to any major NYC hub. I thought that was impossible in this day and age.

Guess you learn something new every day.

I catch my reflection in the rearview mirror and double-check my makeup quickly. Eyeliner and mascara in place, full red lipstick applied, foundation set to battle mode. I'm ready for whatever my hometown has to throw at me. I don't care what the locals here think—my boring, unimaginative, small-minded peers who never bothered to dream past the borders of this town, never imagined any kind of career outside of the same old farming paths their parents and grandparents and great-grandparents trudged down.

They can insult me all they like—same way they did almost two years ago when I came here, straight to the hospital, to hold Mama's hand. They can whisper and elbow each other and smirk behind open palms when I walk past. I don't give a shit because I'm here and then I'm out again.

All I need to do is meet the property assessment manager, find out how much this farm is worth, take a few photos and get it up on a real estate page, then sell it to the first bidder. I don't need the money—I don't care how low the first bid comes in. I'll sell this place for a penny if I need to. I just want to get it off my hands.

My conscience tickles the back of my skull as I think about it.

Okay, fine, maybe I'll do some basic background checking. Make sure that whoever wants to buy it will run it the way it's always been run—as a small, family-run farm, a local business. Not one of these huge Monsanto Corp plots of land my mother was always complaining about. I don't want someone to completely bulldoze the place.

I just want them to take it off my hands and into their own, preferably more capable, hands.

Shouldn't take long. One week, tops. I called into my firm and told them to put my freelance projects on hold for a week. By then I'll be back in my cozy apartment on the Upper East Side, buried in my work once more, happily forgetting that this place ever existed.

You can survive one week, I promise myself. *That's nothing.*

But as I peel into town in the Porsche I rented for this haul (I'm a corporate member, I get free upgrades, so sue me for enjoying the luxury) and immediately draw at least two dozen narrow-eyed stares from the corner café as I whip past toward the narrow road out of town up toward Mama's place, I'm starting to think even a week

16

might be pushing it.

I'm stronger than I think, I remind myself. I survived eighteen years here, after all. Birth all the way up through high school graduation. The girl that grinned through all the insults, glared right back through all the teasing and hair-pulling and muttered comments, fake rumors, bullshit accusations—she's still inside me. Hell, she's the tough-ass bitch who made me successful in NYC.

All I need to do is conjure her up again to survive the next seven days.

I stomp the gas pedal as I leave the town center behind, picking up speed on the bumpy road. I miss this feeling, I have to admit. I don't own a car in the city—that would be stupid, nobody owns a car there. Who would need one?

But there's something liberating about stomping on the gas pedal with no one watching. Flying past the pavement onto the crunching gravel of Mama's longer-than-it-ought-to-be driveway, and not having to take any other cars into consideration.

By the time I reach the house, I'm doing far past any logical speed limit, my heart racing and a huge, stupid grin plastered on my face. Never mind that this car wasn't built for off-roading. Never mind that Mama didn't re-pack the dirt road that makes up the last half-mile or so to the farmstead. It's a rental, I have insurance, I don't care if the undercarriage smacks a few times as I fly over uneven hillocks, then slam on the brakes, nearly skidding right past the driveway into the grass beyond.

I screech to a halt in a billowing cloud of dust, ten feet away from the four-bedroom, single-story wooden farm that I called home for the first eighteen years of my life.

It takes until the dust clears and my adrenaline levels return to normal for me to notice the other occupant of the driveway. The beat-up blue pick-up truck parked on the far side of the house, back to the porch like it's awaiting a delivery of lumber or something practical.

Probably one of the county assessment guys, come to survey the property and figure out how much it's worth. *Crap.* I didn't expect them to beat me here.

It doesn't matter, I remind myself as I put the car in park and grab my Hermès purse—a purse that earns me a million compliments a day back in NYC, but which feels somehow out of place here, too much. I ignore the instincts tickling at the back of my mind. That's just my country self talking. The girl I used to be before I escaped this hellhole.

I face the pickup again and throw my door open. *Who cares what these surveyors think?* And me dusting the place a few times isn't going to make them assess the property value any higher. They'll pay me what they want to pay me for it, no matter what.

I can find a nice charity to donate it to. Something Mama would've loved. I think about those sad-eyed dog commercials on TV, the way she used to tear up every time the music started playing.

I'll look into donating to the ASPCA for her. That would make a nice memorial.

I'm still thinking about sad puppies when I take my first step out of the car… and promptly shriek, toppling forward, barely catching myself on the car door before I face-plant in the mud.

Mud.

Because of course, it rained here last night. And we don't have a cement driveway. Not even a proper gravel one. *"I don't see the sense in splurging on something like that when our trucks can handle this road just fine,"* Mama always said. When I pointed out that sometimes visitors' cars might not be able to navigate the dirt road, she just grinned. *"Exactly. The road weeds 'em out for me."*

Mama was never big on strangers visiting. Hell, even when friends popped by to visit, she always needed alone time to recharge after they left. The ultimate introvert.

I pull my high heels out of the mud with a horrible sucking sound and teeter on them while I slam the door closed. Dammit. A perfectly good pair of Luis Vuittons caked in country muck. At least I was smart enough not to wear the suede boots I almost put on this morning, dressing for my flight at the crack of dawn. These are leather—I have hope the mud will wash off.

I shoulder my purse once more, square my shoulders, and face the short walk to the porch.

Shit.

Now that I'm looking at the house head-on, it looks a lot more run-down than I remember. I didn't stop by last time I was here—I just went straight to Mama's hospital bed, and stayed in the hotel next door the whole visit. It's been fifteen years since I last stood in this driveway. Since I hopped into my crappy pickup truck, just barely holding itself together long enough for one last road trip. Since I filled the truck bed with my every worldly possession, kissed Mama goodbye and drove three days straight to NYC. Since I stomped on that gas pedal and never looked back.

I take a halting step toward the house, my mind more full of images of the way it used to look than the dilapidated structure before my eyes. I spot the tire swing out front, the one Mama had our neighbor Beck hang for me. Shockingly, it's still there, the worn rope he used to hang it apparently a hell of a lot thicker and sturdier than it looked.

Past the tire swing, a few of the apple trees out front have sickened and died. They're still upright, hanging on just barely. I'll need to cut those down, I know, before a storm passes through and sends them crashing down on their own, wreaking more havoc. At least I can chop up the wood, fill the wood shed out back and have more than enough to spare for winter, when the wood-burning stove in the kitchen eats pine by the belly-full.

Then I stop and shake myself. What am I talking about? I'm going to be back home by winter. Safe and snug in my apartment, rent paid, utilities included, any breaks or wear and tear the landlord's problem, not mine.

I push open the rickety front gate, which shrieks on rusty metal hinges, and then shriek myself as I promptly fall in an ankle-deep hole. Luckily I catch myself on the gate before I hit the ground, but it's enough to make me grit my teeth in frustration, reach down and, despite the early fall chill in the dirt, yank off my heels, one after the other.

That's quite enough of that.

Heels in hand, I stretch my ankle — feels fine, thank goodness — and step around the gate, eyes now warily fixed on the ground. There are holes everywhere — something burrowing has taken up residence in what used to be our front walk.

Something like guilt tugs at me. I probably shouldn't have left this place so long untended. I should have come down to take care of selling it off the moment Mama passed away, instead of letting it sit around waiting for me.

Regardless of the guilt, though, what rises faster and starker in my mind is revulsion. I hate it here. Always have, always will. Everything from that ugly tire swing to the stupid gate to the sagging porch out front and the weather-worn paint on the windows in a color that used to be cheery but is now just another depressing reminder of how dead this farm is.

It died with Mama, and along with her died any last reason I might ever have had to feel sentimental about this grubby old shack.

I cross to the porch, planning to go inside — might as well get the worst over with. That's when I hear a deafening cracking sound, followed by two wooden clatters. After a pause, I hear it again, and it resolves into a familiar noise.

Someone is chopping wood out back.

I frown. Not exactly the type of activity I expect to find my property assessor engaged in.

Then again, country folk are strange. Maybe he wanted to take home some bits of one of the dead trees as a souvenir.

I abandon the front door for now and follow the hole-pitted path around back, ignoring the way the semi-hard mud squishes underneath my toes and the occasional rock that jabs against my bare soles. I used to have tough feet, the kind I could run straight across gravel with. Now I'm a tenderfoot again, wincing at every stray pebble.

It only makes my resentment grow. I've grown strong in other ways since I left this farm. I built a life for myself, a career I'm proud of. A career that keeps me up all night and then again first thing in the morning, burning the candle at both ends, but still.

I round the edge of the house and stop dead on the path, forgetting for a moment about my rage. Hell, even about the pebbles I'm standing on.

In front of me, shirtless and sheened in sweat, is the most perfectly sculpted man I have ever seen.

He could be made of bronze the way he's posing now, weighing the axe over his shoulder as he eyes the stack of wood in front of him, balanced on the same tree stump where my Mama used to chop her own wood years ago. I can count every single muscle on his chest, from his pecs down his washboard abs to the perfect V that points like an arrow straight down, to a faint line of dark hair that I can't help tracing to the fly of his jeans.

Damn jeans.

It takes every ounce of my self-control not to drool when he swings the axe all over again, distracting me with the surge and flow of his biceps, the way even his back ripples with strength. He's got longer hair than I'm typically into, bound in a tight bun at the nape of his neck, dark and curly, to judge by the few flyaways that have escaped the hair tie.

I'm still gawking when he turns to look at me.

Holy shit. No way.

My jaw threatens to drop completely open because I realize—only when he looks straight at me head—I *know* this guy.

Grant Werther. The formerly scrawny kid who used to chase me around this lawn every summer while our parents talked shop. His dad owned a farm up the road, had the same business problems to deal with as Mom.

I have to say, he's filled out nicely. His face, which used to be all thin angles, now features sharp cheekbones, a cut jaw and a fine nose. His eyes are dark too, piercing where they catch mine and lock, and his dark, full beard only accentuates his looks.

I swallow so hard I nearly gulp down my tongue in the process.

As for him, he shows no signs of recognizing me at all. Fine, if he wants to play at that game. "What are you doing here?" I manage to ask, finally recovering my wits.

"I could ask you the same thing." He runs a hand over his hair, taming a few of those wisps, and narrows his eyes. "This is private property, Miss."

Miss. So he really doesn't recognize me. How is that possible? We hung out every summer until we hit high school. Until he started hanging with the cool athletic crowd and left me in the dust.

He keeps his voice cold and formal, but I don't miss the way his gaze drops over my body, lingering on my chest and my hips. I dressed the same way I do every day this morning — to kill. The tight pencil skirt and the designer top that hugs me just close enough to display a hint of my curves isn't the worst thing I could be caught wearing by a handsome blast from the past. Serves him right for not putting the pieces together. If he's on this farm, he has to have some inkling of my identity. Doesn't he?

I shake myself back to reality. *What am I thinking?* This jerk is trying to order me off my own lawn. I don't give a damn if he remembers me or finds me attractive.

"No shit it is," I reply, shifting my hands to my hips and drawing myself up to my full height. I'd be taller with the damned heels on, but... "It's *my* private property, so I'll ask you again. What are you doing here?"

"I have just as much rights to this land as you do, Sasha."

The sound of my name stuns me silent for a second. Okay. Maybe I was wrong. Maybe he does still have a few fond memories of me.

Then he keeps talking and spoils the illusion. "That is who you are, right? Sasha Bluebell, only ungrateful daughter of Maryanne Bluebell?"

Okay. That does it. I ball my fists. "Listen, Mister —"

"Grant Werther," he answers, butting across me.

I laugh that off. He thinks I'm as forgetful as him? Fine. "You can't just come storming in here acting like you own the place. I have the deed to this land —"

"And half of that deed belongs to me, you'll find."

That draws me up short. I finally process what he said earlier, before my name. *I have just as much rights to this land as you do.* What does *that* mean?

Grant wipes his palms on his jeans and reaches into his back pocket. There's a rustle as he unfolds a piece of paper, then crosses the grass to my side, paper extended before him.

I accept it with a pointed glare.

"My father loaned your mother money seventeen years ago," he's saying. "In exchange for 50% ownership of the farm."

I ignore him and skim the paper instead. Dealing with Mama's accounts has left me better versed in legalese than I'd like to be. But unfortunately, the contract in front of me, signed and notarized in Mama's unique handwriting, agrees with everything he's saying.

"Pop left me his share when he passed," Grant is saying, his tone irritatingly arrogant. "Which means I own his half."

I refold the paper, mouth pressed into a thin line. I don't want to admit he's right. I don't want to concede defeat. So I just pass him back the paper and fix him with another long glare. "Fine. So we're both part owners. That doesn't mean you can stand here on the lawn where I grew up and insinuate things about my relationship with my Mama or act like you know the first damned thing about me."

His eyebrows rise, just a little.

"Ungrateful daughter," I say, for emphasis, in case he forgot the insult.

But far from looking reprimanded or taught his place, he only seems to look more… amused. "That's me told, then," is all Grant says.

For some reason, that irritates me even more. I cross my arms and lean on one leg, heels still dangling from one hand. His gaze darts to the shoes in my fist, then my bare feet, but if he has anything to remark about my state, at least he keeps it to himself. "What's your intention with your half of the share?" I ask. "Because my plan is to clean the place up as best I can, as fast as I can, and then sell it for whatever I can get."

He tears his gaze from me at last — an event that both relieves and frustrates me at the same time, for reasons I don't want to think too hard about — and eyes the house behind me. For a moment, it seems like there's something else in his expression. A cloud I can't quite read or understand. Then he shakes his head. "Clean the place up. Sell it for whatever we can get, once we're ready. Sounds good to me."

I press my mouth into a thin line, even as relief floods me. At least he wants the same thing I do. "Good," I reply. "Then we're agreed. We have the same goal, make this place look as good as she possibly can, and sell her to the highest bidder. Equal split to both of us for whatever we make."

He nods.

"That makes us partners, then," I continue. "We should work together."

A short, cursory laugh escapes him then. He glances at me once more, but this time his gaze lingers on my heels, my skirt, my bare, pale feet which haven't seen sunlight since my last beach trip, way back at the beginning of the summer because I never found time to go again. "I doubt *you* can do much work at all," he replies, smirking.

I toss my head, shoulders squared. "Oh? And you're basing this opinion of me on what, exactly? Whatever bullshit town gossip you've clearly swallowed hook line and sinker?"

He shrugs, not bothering to deny it. "Generally when enough people believe something, they have a decent reason."

"So you just always believe the mob mentality about a new person, no matter what it is?" *Or even a person you* used *to know?*

"People around here always said you looked down on us. Hated the country life, and not just the life, but also anyone who wanted that life for themselves. They say you thought you were too good for this town and everyone in it — that's why you turned heel and never once looked back."

I laugh once, soft and bitter. "Who knows? Maybe they're right after all," I mutter. "I certainly am too good for *this,*" I add with a glance at my now mud-spattered feet.

"If the golden shoe fits…" Grant shrugs again.

"I earned that shoe, I'll have you know," I snap.

"Never meant to imply you didn't," he replies easily, yet somehow it feels like another snub. I side-eye him as he bends down to collect the wood he's chopped — a small, tidy pile that'll be just enough for the stove to last a day or two. When he straightens again, wood cradled in his arms, he raises a single eloquent eyebrow. "Well? You want to see the interior?"

I grimace. "Depends. Is it as shabby as this yard?"

His mouth flat lines again. "It's just a little overgrowth."

"Are you kidding?" I blurt, flinging my arms wide. "There's at least three dead trees out front, potholes everywhere, the gate's rusting down, that tire swing could probably kill anyone unlucky enough to set foot on it..."

"Superficial," he contradicts. "Won't take more than a week to clear."

"It better not. I want to be out of this hellhole by next weekend, not a minute later."

Any potential friendship I might have noticed budding in his expression dies out again. "And you wonder why people think you're stuck-up, Sasha," he mutters. Yet he glances sidelong at me as he says it, his eyes lingering just a little too long on my chest to be excusable. He's into me. It's obvious.

And to my surprise, despite my annoyance at him — no, more than annoyance, it's borderline anger now —I realize that my gaze keeps doing the same. Tracing those biceps, that flat plane of stomach, now pressed against the bundle of wood he's holding. Oh, to be that pile of wood…

I shake myself. That's insane. And he's not my type anyway. He's way too big, in every sense of the word. Big muscled, big as in way taller than me — *probably has a big dick,* my mind unhelpfully points out.

But he's also got an incurable case of huge ego. So, no, thank you.

"I don't wonder," I respond with a toss of my hair. "I know." It's easy to play the villain they all believe me to be. The jerk city girl who's come to laugh at all the farm kids. It's easy because I've been in their shoes. I know how much I hated it. I've made myself a different life, and I'm not ashamed of it. These country folk aren't going to make me feel that way, either. No matter how many rumors they start.

Grant casts one last long, searching look at me, then scoffs deep in the back of his throat. Disapproving. Dismissing. He shakes his head and storms past me. I watch his back as he climbs the back steps into the house and shoulders open the door. Annoyed as I am, I can't help admitting that I like the view as he goes.

As soon as the door slams between us, I exhale in relief. Well. That was unexpected.

Unexpected, unpleasant. This town is already living up to my memories and then some.

Right, I remind myself. I'm here because I have a job to do. So, first things first, I'm going to accomplish that job.

I turn my back on the house for now. First things first means securing myself a bed to sleep in tonight that won't feature moth-eaten bedding and a moldy mattress. As I climb back into the car, though, I can't help glancing back at the house one last time. I notice a twitch in the living room curtains.

Grant, no doubt, watching me drive away again. Well, good. Let him sit in there and stew. Hopefully by the time I get back, he'll have a better attitude about this whole mess.

"Yes, a room for one," I repeat.

"I'm sorry, Ms. Bluebell. We simply don't have space." The hotel clerk stares at me blandly across the desk.

Calling him a clerk seems a little much. He's the lone employee at the only hotel in town, a three story building next to the hospital, the same one I stayed in while I was visiting Mama.

I check for a name tag so I can plead with him on a first name basis. But he's not wearing one. Dammit. What *was* his name? I'm not used to having to remember those sorts of details. Not anymore. Did it start with an M? R?

"I'll take any size. Double or triple, I'll pay the extra, I don't mind."

"We don't have any rooms available, I'm afraid."

"Really, this is just…" I fling my hands up. "The sign out front says Vacancy. That's false advertising if there isn't a room."

"You'll have to take that up with the owner," he replies with a bland smile. His eyes, though, burn bright with mockery.

I have a sinking, suspicious feeling that *he* is the owner. But, of course, I can't call him on it. Because I don't remember — I blocked out every detail of this damn town as fast as possible. So I just have to grimace and heave a sigh. "Thanks anyway," I mumble as I turn tail, defeated.

"Best of luck," he replies in a bubbly, friendly way that makes it sound exactly like *go fuck yourself.*

"You too," I call back, bright and bubbly. Hope he takes the same meaning from my words, too.

I checked all the online rental sites — no response to the three Airbnb requests I sent out, but if this hotel counter guy is anything to judge by, all three of those owners will have the same answer for me.

The next closest hotel is a two-hour drive out of town. Way too far for me to make every day this week if I want to make serious headway on the house.

There's nothing left for it. I climb back into my rental car and turn back toward the farm.

Chapter 3

Grant Werther

She doesn't remember me.

For a moment, I thought. When I first caught her staring, pretended not to notice and kept chopping. I thought the neurons might be firing, catching her up. But the moment she spoke, I knew. There was no recognition in her tone, no hint of happiness.

It's only been sixteen years, Sasha. The least you could do is remember me.

But what did I expect? A sudden role-reversal from the town's infamous prodigal daughter?

I should have known.

I *did* know, deep down. From the moment I first found the agreement in Pop's old documents. I started work on this place right away because I knew she'd be no help — if she even bothered to show her face here. Now, weeks after I started in on this spot, already going through the basement and the worst of the foundations, Her Highness finally decides so show her face. And the first thing she does is try to kick me off the farm?

Adding insult to injury.

I shove it to the back of my mind. Doesn't matter. I finish this job, then I get half the money for this place. It'll be more than enough to finish the add-ons I want to make at Pop's farm. More than enough to keep his legacy going, even though it'll be one of the last family-owned farms left in this town.

Sasha Bluebell does not matter, I remind myself. Not one bit.

It doesn't matter that she grew up even more stunning than she used to be at eleven, chasing me around this backyard with legs as long as a doe's. It doesn't matter that despite her fancy expensive designer clothes, she's still got those curves I remember her showing hints of as a teenager, right before she left. Those sexy hips and full breasts, separated by a waist I would kill to wrap my hands around. Her lips; those look exactly the same. Those bowstring lips I used to close my eyes and picture every night from age ten on. And her eyes have gone a darker, deeper green. The kind of backyard, nature green you could lose yourself in for hours. I did, once. We used to lie in this very backyard at dusk and count bats. Then wait until moonrise and count stars instead. Only I'd count more than just stars. I'd count how many seconds I could get away with watching her before she turned her head and caught me. Before she'd scowl and swat my arm and tell me to stop being so weird.

Before our hands would brush, tangle, just for a second, and then she'd leap away again, change the subject.

I never knew if she thought the same things I did. I assumed so, I figured there was no way she couldn't feel it too, the tension thrumming in the air between us, making the sweltering hot country summer nights even hotter with unspoken desire.

But I guess I was wrong. If she doesn't even remember my name now, then, well...

I scowl and finish chopping the last round of wood I'll need for the next few nights. I could commute from Pop's, but it's a long drive to make each way daily, especially when I want to be up and at it first thing here. I cleaned up the single bedroom and have been camping out in it since last week when I realized I'd need to ramp up my speed on this fixer-upper if I wanted to get her on the market before winter hits and does any more damage. It's not that the house herself is doing bad — she's got good bones underneath it all. But that's not normally what potential buyers look at. It's all first impressions with them, window dressing. So I need to do that up as nice as possible if I want to earn enough to keep Pop's farm going.

Which means I need to keep my head in the damn game.

I'm rewiring the lighting in the living room, which needs some work, when I hear tires out front. A door slams, and then I hear the unmistakable cursing of a city girl who's not used to getting a little mud on her heels. I resist the urge to check the window. I don't know where Sasha drove off to earlier, and I don't care. She's none of my business.

I'm elbow-deep in the wall when she crashes through the front door.

"I cannot believe some —" Sasha stops dead when she sees what I'm doing. "Is that safe?" She's squinting at the electrical panel hanging open next to me.

I ignore her and finish adjusting the last two fuses. Then I step back and flip a switch. Light floods the living room — and, though you can't see it from here, the kitchen and bedroom too. An improvement over before, when only the kitchen power was working, and even then it was choppy.

"Oh," she replies, answering her own question as she blinks at the lights. "Are you an electrician or…?"

"Just picked up a few things," I reply. "Happens when you live in a hellhole, I guess."

She bites her lip. It draws my eye, irresistible. Not to mention starts an unwelcome stirring against my jeans… Damn. I want to be the one biting that sexy lip. "Listen, Grant, I'm sorry about earlier. I was a little…" She shakes her head. "It was a long flight. Then a long drive. And people have been so weird to me here. Like at the hotel just now, there were clearly about a dozen vacant rooms, and they told me it was full."

"Mark does tend to harbor a grudge," I reply, fairly. "If you didn't give him an online review last visit, he gets a bit snippy."

Her cheeks flush. That is more than a little distracting too. So she blushes easily, good to know. I wonder what else I could do to make her blush….

I'm getting harder just thinking about all the ways to make this innocent city girl turn bright red.

"Mark. Dammit, I knew it was an M name."

I laugh. "If you didn't even remember his name, you're doomed."

"What do I do?" She frowns and glances past me at the living room. There's something in her eye, something honestly and truly panicked that makes me almost feel bad for her.

Almost.

"I can't stay here," she blurts.

"I'll talk to Mark," I promise her. Her eyes immediately go wide with relief. I hold up a hand to stave it off. "But he's not going to be around anymore at this hour. You'll have to rough it one night here, Princess."

Her cheeks flare again. "I'll take my old room," she murmurs, starting for the hallway off the kitchen, the one that leads to the tinier spare room. I'm surprised she even remembered where that was.

But I have to cut her off. "Your Mama turned that into an office a few years back."

Sasha stumbles to a halt. Fuck, even her confused face is sexy. "So…" She trails off, leaves that question unspoken.

"There's your Mama's room." I let that hang long enough for her eyes to go wide yet again. But they're still fixed dead on mine—she doesn't back down from a challenge.

I guess some things, at least, haven't changed.

"I'll sleep in the car," she says, hands on her hips.

I smirk. "What's the matter, scared to be too near one of us country hicks?"

Our eyes lock. That wipes any remaining politeness from her expression. Good. I always preferred her when she was angry. The way her eyebrows crease and her fists ball, the way she won't back down from a fight. The way she's glaring at me right now, though, is making me harder still.

Fuck. How am I still so fucking attracted to her, after all these years?

"Of course not," she replies, chin high. "I'm only being polite. You take the bed."

I step closer. She holds her ground. I catch a whiff of her perfume now, something floral, expensive I'd guess. It smells okay, great probably. But I like her better without it. I like *her* scent, the one that's all Sasha, can't be bottled. "We could always share." I grin at the way that sets off a white hot flush across her cheeks. Then I turn away from her, still smiling to myself. "But that's okay. Don't want to make you nervous, city girl. You couldn't handle a wild man like me anyway."

She snorts. "Oh, I doubt that."

"Is that a challenge?" I turn back to raise one eyebrow at her, and find she's moved closer to me, almost chasing me, fists still clenched.

Fuck, she's glorious when she's annoyed.

She holds my gaze for a long moment. Long enough that I know she's thinking about it. About what fucking me would be like.

Good. Let her dream. Let her be the one to lie awake at night and fantasize, for once.

"You take the bed," I tell her, hands spread in what I hope comes across as the peace offering I mean it to be. "My truck bed is bigger than your Porsche's backseat anyway. And I've got a quilt in the truck from other times I've roughed it."

She opens her mouth, though whether to agree or decline the favor, I don't stick around to find out. I dust off my palms, leave her with the firewood, and head outside to make my bed for the night.

Chapter 4

Sasha Bluebell

The sound of hammering wakes me up. Well, that and the rooster crying away in some far off field. I crack one eyelid at my blinds, then groan and fling an arm over my forehead to shade myself from the dawn light beginning to tint the blinds.

What time is it?

My phone, down to its last cell of battery life since I couldn't find a plug near the bed in this tiny room—how on earth did Mama sleep without her cell phone beside her?—tells me it's 5:04am. Not the kind of hour any civilized person should ever greet from this side of sleep.

But the hammering continues, directly overhead and growing louder by the minute. And unless I'm much mistaken, I do catch a whiff of something at least somewhat promising in the air.

Coffee.

I stumble out of the bedroom wiping sleep from my eyes to find a fresh pot of coffee on the stove and a little plate of toast and jam waiting beside it. I munch on the toast while I tie my hair into some semblance of a bun, then pull on a pair of jean shorts and toss on the only tank top I packed. Normally this would be a running shirt, but I'm working with what I've got for now. At least I remembered to bring a pair of boots. Granted, they're leather, but they're sturdy work boots, not the heels I stupidly put on yesterday morning. I yank them on too, and I'm surprised how good it feels to be wearing sturdy, reliable shoes.

Must be because I'm still feeling grumpy about tripping in the mud yesterday.

That finished, I splash my face clean, then bring my coffee outside to see about the racket.

Grant is on the roof. I lean back to squint at his broad, muscular back—unfortunately clothed today—and watch him lay out another roof tile, then hammer it into place. He's about halfway done reshingling the roof, to judge from here.

"Need a hand?" I call up.

He turns around to squint down at me with what's clearly doubt in his eyes.

That only makes me want to prove him wrong the more. He thinks he knows me—spoiled city girl, the town stuck-up bitch. Well, I might be a city girl now, but I was born country. Some things you don't forget how to do.

Clearly, he doesn't remember the way we used to clamber up every tree in the woods around here. Or the tree house we built, us and a couple of our neighborhood friends, with our own hands. It's been a while, but I can still swing a hammer, thank-you-very-much Grant.

I set my coffee down and climb onto the ladder. He watches with progressively wider eyes as I scurry right up it to join him. I don't even pause when I switch onto the roof and keep my balance easily as I cross it to his side.

To his credit, he doesn't dismiss me the way

some guys might. He just passes me a hammer from the tool bag perched beside him. I accept it, and our hands graze for a moment, his calloused skin rough against mine, like a match striking. It sets my whole body on fire, and I have to turn away for a second to catch my breath, to drive out the sudden images flashing in my mind.

Him shirtless yesterday, glistening with sweat.

His eyes, the way they bore into mine, dark and serious.

How those eyes and that sexy shirtless body of his would look above me in a dark room as he tossed me down onto the single bed in this house and...

I shake myself back into the present.

"You know how to use this thing?" he says.

"Might need a refresher course," I reply. "It's been a while."

He grabs some nails as well, and holds up another roof tile for me. As he demonstrates how to grip the hammer, reaching around me to do so, I nearly lose my grip in distraction. *Fuck.* He smells amazing. The sweat he's worked up already makes his scent even more noticeable—something piney with a heady undertone that's all him, a hint of salt that makes me lick my lips unconsciously. He presses against me, and his hand wraps around mine around the hammer, that rough skin so firm against mine, his hand so strong, and *huge*. It completely engulfs my hand.

His whole body, to be honest, is huge. So much bigger than the scrawny kid I remember. Or even the handsome but lean guy in high school who never so much as glanced my way, despite all the summers we spent together as kids. Now, with the way he's built up… God, he could toss me around the bedroom any way he wanted.

Fuck. Stop it, Sasha. This is not the time or the place.

"Paying attention?" he asks, his voice low and close to my ear—so close the breath tickles my skin.

Dammit. "Of course," I respond.

He lines up the first nail, shows me how to drive it in. Then he shows me what angle to lay the next tile so the roof will all lie flat and orderly. Then he releases me, and I try to ignore the quiver in my thighs, or the way my pussy tightens in reflexive protest.

Having him kneeling behind me was too damn hot.

I suck in fresh air to try to clear my head, and then, while he watches, I nail down another tile, then another.

Eventually, he nods, satisfied, and goes back to his own pile of tiles.

I try not to watch him out of the corner of my eye too often. Or to track the way his biceps flex as he drives in the hammer.

Once or twice, I catch him looking back at me. My cheeks flush both times, and by the third time, I tell myself I need to behave. I keep my eyes ahead, focused on the tiles, and shift over ahead of him. That way I won't be tempted.

We work in tandem for what feels like hours, though to judge by the way the sun is inching up the horizon, it can't be more than one hour at most. I make it all the way up to the center of the roof, and then I turn to get more tiles.

This time, though, it's Grant who I find staring at me. More specifically, at my ass. My cheeks flush again, and I realize with how short these shorts are, and how far I'm bent over kneeling on this roof, my ass cheeks must have been showing.

I set down the hammer, face bright red. "If I'm distracting you, you know, I can go and change," I say, mostly to call him out. Even though, I have to admit, I'm enjoying knowing the effect I have on this guy. He might be judgmental at times, but he's also hot as hell. It's been a long time. Good to know I've still got it.

Grant's eyes catch mine, full of humor. But

his voice is dead serious when he replies, "Don't."

That one word makes my belly clench, and my legs quiver. Combined with the way his dark eyes still hook on mine, boring into me, it's making the ache between my legs grow to a distracting level.

Then he smirks again, a knowing smile that tells me he knows just how much of an effect he's having on me. Without another word, he turns back to his own work.

After a moment's hesitation, I go back to nailing down my row of shingles too. We work until almost half the roof is finished, when Grant leans back on his heels and taps the empty bucket. "Out of nails. I'll have to do a supply run later."

"I can go," I offer.

"Do you even remember where the hardware store is?" He cocks an eyebrow.

I bite my lip. "I have GPS."

"You think any stores in this town are on Google Maps?" He laughs.

59

I sigh and sit back on my heels. "Still. If you give me directions, I don't mind running out. You've put in so much work here already." I cast an eye past the rooftop, at the distant yard, where, from this vantage, I've already been able to see evidence of his handiwork. Some of the fields have been plowed, the soil tilled. Others show signs of recent plantings. Not only is he fixing up the house itself, but he's even working on the land. I didn't even think to do that. "I want to pull my own weight."

"Clearly you can," he replies, casting a glance at the tiles I lined up. "My mistake for doubting you."

"I accept your apology," I answer with a faint smile.

He grins back at me. "Still don't think you can handle everything about country life, City Girl."

"You mean life in general or something in particular?" I lift one eyebrow.

"I was thinking selfishly, I'll admit."

"And just why do you think I can't handle

60

you, exactly, Country Boy?"

His gaze drops over my body again, slowly. "You turn bright red every time I look at you, let alone say anything."

He's right, I am blushing. But I force myself to lift my chin and lock eyes with him. I want to prove him wrong. I'm not the blushing girl he thinks. "Why, have something you want to say?"

"Plenty, Sasha."

My pussy clenches noticeably at the sound of my name in his mouth. Fuck. Why does he know how to turn me on so easily? "So go for it, Grant," I reply. I raise my brows, inviting.

But he just shakes his head and turns to reach for the ladder down. "I'm going to clean up. Then I'll do a hardware store run. Feel free to tag along if you want to know where it is."

Before I can even reply, he's down the ladder, leaving me alone on the rooftop, wondering what on earth just happened.

Half an hour later, I've made it down from the roof too and dusted myself off. I head into the bedroom to grab my stuff and go change. But when I pass the lone bathroom in the farmhouse, the steam escaping through the open door catches my eye. It's only opened a crack, just a couple inches. But it's enough to glimpse, via the mirror hanging over the sink, a reflection of what's happening in the shower.

I should keep walking. I *know* I should. But my feet have their own idea. They slow, stumble to a halt before the door, and, unable to help myself, I steal a peek through the open doorway.

At first all I see is shower tile. I'm about to take a deep breath, tear my gaze away and turn toward the bedroom instead, when movement catches my eye. Grant steps into view, reaching for something on the other side of the narrow shower.

He's turned to the side, giving me a glimpse of muscular thighs, and an ass so tight and round it makes my stomach clench and my mouth water. But then he turns back toward the shower again, and my jaw drops.

He *is* a big man. Huge, in fact.

He's not even hard right now, I think in shock, at the sight of his thick cock. I can't imagine what it would be like to be fucked by a man like him. I've never been with anyone that big. But my pussy tenses, my panties damp. Clearly my body wants to find out.

Too bad, I scold it. I spin away from the door and hurry toward the bedroom before I get caught gawking at someone I should definitely not be fantasizing about. But the whole time I shrug out of my tank top and into a clean shirt for our run into town, I can't stop picturing his body. The water from the shower curling down over his taut muscles. I imagine being in that shower with him. The way he'd pin me against the wall and lift me off my feet easily, like I weighed nothing at all. The way he'd thrust into me, and how thick he'd feel inside my tight pussy, stretching me out, making me scream with pleasure…

Stop thinking about it, Sasha. Clearly I'm just horny. It's been a long time since my last hookup. That's the only explanation I can think of for why I'd suddenly be so into a guy like this, a guy so different from my usual type. I like pretty nerdy boys. The kind of guys I can have a long intellectual conversation with before we make love to our favorite soundtrack. Not guys like this.

Not guys who could probably fuck me harder than I've ever been fucked before.

I force that thought, along with all the rest, from my mind. Force them out and focus on what I need to do now—go finish our errands for the day.

I straighten my fresh shirt and consider my jean shorts for a second. I could change them. But I'm remembering Grant's eyes on my ass, and the way he smirked at me. That one word he uttered.

Don't.

So I leave the shorts on, grab my wallet, and head out into the living room.

When I get there, Grant is already dressed and waiting for me. I resist the urge to glance at his crotch, wondering if I'd be able to see the outline of his cock through those jeans. *Wondering what it would take to get him hard for me.*

I can't think like that. I'm too distracted as it is.

For his part, Grant just smiles when he sees me, ambiguous, hard-to-read. Is he smirking at me, or does he just always look a little bit haughty, like he knows something I don't?

"Ready?" he asks.

I nod, and he leads us out toward the cars. He bypasses mine straightaway—and I can't exactly complain. The dirt roads aren't too helpful on this rental's undercarriage. He heads straight for his truck and I trail after him.

Then we nearly collide because he's stopped

in front of the passenger door to open it for me.

"Oh, I can…" I reach for the handle then pause halfway. Because he's shaking his head.

"I might be a country boy, but I was raised with manners," he says. He opens the door and swings it open, then steps aside while extending a hand.

I glance from the truck to him and back again. The step is two feet off the ground—nothing I couldn't handle with effort, but still. I place my hand in his, and thrill at the warmth of his skin, the strength in his hands. I lean on him as I step up, and he lifts me easily toward the cabin as I climb into the passenger side seat.

He shuts the door behind me and circles around to his side of the truck while I'm still catching my breath from that touch. *Dammit.* Why does he have such an effect?

He climbs into the driver's seat and shuts the door, not bothering with a seatbelt as the turns the ignition. Country music blares over his loud speakers, but louder than that is the growl in the truck's engine, itching to be gassed.

Just the sound of the truck motor—a real engine—brings back a flood of memories. Riding shotgun with Mama into town for groceries, bouncing on the seat with every bump to make the ride feel like a roller coaster at the county fair.

Learning how to drive myself on these roads, gunning it as fast as I could so I could feel like I was flying—flying away from all this.

Riding shotgun with Dad, back before—No. I cut that memory off short. I don't think about those days.

I run a hand across the dashboard, unable to conceal my smile.

"Been a while since you've been taken for a real ride, has it?" Grant asks, a wide smirk on his face. I'm not sure if he's talking about the truck, exactly. My face flushes.

"Might be," I admit.

"Well. Might want to buckle up then," he

replies, grinning.

Without further warning, he guns it. We're facing down the driveway, but even though I just drove up and down this twice yesterday, it feels completely different from here. From the seat in a truck built for this terrain, driven by someone who knows how to handle these country roads. Pretty soon we pick up enough speed to barrel along, and I whoop, unable to contain my elation.

Grant laughs. "You need to loosen up once in a while, City Girl," he calls over the roar of the road under our tires, the rush of wind through the cracked windows, because of course this thing doesn't even have air con. And for some reason I don't even mind. "You're a lot more fun this way."

"Yeah, well you're a lot more fun when you're taking me for a ride instead of calling me names," I shout back with a smirk.

He lifts an eyebrow at that. "Can't I do both?"

"Guess that depends on what kind of names

you plan to call me," I shout back, just as we reach the end of the driveway and he slows down, enough that my voice echoes in the cabin.

Grant barks out a laugh. "Oh, I can think of a fair few that'd suit you, City Girl." He glances over at me, and his eyes do that thing again, that slow wander across my body that sets every nerve ending on fire.

"I'm working on a list of my own for you, Country Boy."

"Still think you can handle this, do you." He doesn't say it like a question. He says it like a challenge, a dare. At the same time, he turns onto the main road toward town, not meeting my eye anymore.

"I like a challenge," I reply, chin lifted.

"Hm. Careful what you wish for," he answers to that, casting one last sideways glance at me before he turns his attention to the road.

For a few moments we fall silent, listening to the upbeat country tune that's currently pounding in his speakers. It's one I recognize, one I forgot I even knew the words to, and I find myself mouthing them under my breath as we roll through town.

Just like yesterday when I first drove in—and in the afternoon when I rode down to talk to Mark at the hotel—all eyes are on us once more. But this time, as we drive through the town square, the center of town, the social hangout for everyone and their parents—and their grandparents too, for that matter—I sense a difference. This time, I notice far more girls turning to eyeball the truck, following its path, their eyes eagerly searching out the driver's seat.

And I notice more than a few of those smiles shifting into frowns when their eyes wander past the driver's seat toward the passenger side and finding it occupied.

Well. Can't blame them. I'd be thirsty for a guy like Grant too, if all I had to choose from were the pickings in this small town.

You're hungry for him even when you do

have more options, the unhelpful voice in the back of my head points out.

I bite the inside of my cheek to stop myself from fantasizing again. But that's hard when the whole cab of this truck smells like him. When his warm body is just a couple feet away from mine, his arm muscles bulging as he shifts the truck down a gear and turns away from the plaza.

"Are you paying attention?" he asks, and I startle, tearing my gaze from his biceps.

"Hmm?"

"You wanted to know how to get to the hardware store, didn't you?" He rolls his eyes, but he's smirking too. He's enjoying how distracting he is, damn him.

I lean back in my seat. "Right." I force my eyes on the road. Force my mind to stop imagining how it would feel if he swung this truck into a parking spot and used those thick, strong hands to reach for me instead of the gearshift. I'd bet he could pull me onto his lap before I even had time to gasp and tell him it was improper in public.

Then I imagine what *that* would feel like—
kneeling across him while he wraps those strong
hands around my firm ass and pulls me down into
his lap. I picture the bulge in his jeans from thick
cock; imagine grinding myself against him... *Fuck,*
I could probably get off on that alone, like a horny
teenager.

"You're drifting again," he points out, and I
blink, startled to realize we've already gone three
more streets while I wasn't looking.

"No, I'm not," I protest.

"Sure. And we're where, again?"

I lick my lips. Frown. "I'm not great with
directions," I protest.

"Uh huh." He swings a left in front of a site
I do recognize, though—the church Mama used to
go to. The church I went to growing up, and that
helps me orient myself.

So many of the other stores have changed.
Call me naive, but I'd have thought that in a little

town like this, the big chain stores wouldn't make much of a dent. But I spot a Starbucks on one corner and an IHOP across the way, and frown.

"Where'd Billy's go?" I ask, before I think better of it. Before I realize that's a memory lane I don't want to ride down. Fraught with all the things I remember after mass, heading there every Sunday for pancakes and coffee with—*No.*

"Not such a bad sense of direction after all." Grant shakes his head with a sigh. "Billy's closed down about ten years back. After Billy passed. Neither of his sons wanted to keep the place running. Rick tried to sell it for a while, but…" He shrugged one shoulder. "Not many people into the small town life these days. Everyone wants to run away to the big city. Forget their roots where they buried them." He shoots me a sideways glance at that, and I clamp my mouth into a thin line.

"As long as they're doing what they enjoy, don't think you ought to blame them," I say.

"Course not," he says. "As long as it's really

what they enjoy."

With that enigmatic statement, Grant pulls into the parking lot attached to *Tulip Hardware*, just a couple blocks up from where Billy's used to be. At least that'll be easy enough for me to remember.

We head inside, and Grant gives me a list of supplies to find while he hunts down the rest of the things we need. I manage to locate the nails we'll need to finish the roof, as well as the various yard tools that have either rusted away or been borrowed from our shed and never returned in Mama's absence.

I beat Grant to the counter and find an older couple chatting behind it. Their gazes slide over to me, at first with an absent glance, then narrowing in recognition and suspicion, in a way I'm getting used to spotting.

These people must know me. Or knew Mama, at any rate.

"Can we help you?" the man asks, a bite in his tone.

The woman doesn't say anything, just stares.

"Er, I wanted to buy these." I place the items on the counter.

He eyes them doubtfully. Doesn't make a move to stand or start checking me out yet, though.

The woman leans over to pick up a cup of coffee from its perch on a neighboring stack of books and sips it politely for a long moment.

I stand there watching, eyes wide. Are they really just going to ignore me?

But after a long, almost never-ending moment, the woman finally sighs and pushes to her feet, grumbling like I'm asking the biggest, most interminable task of her. "Thirty for the lot," she pronounces, without even looking at what I've laid on the table.

"But…" I bite my lip. I did the math already. None of this should add up to more than twenty bucks at most.

"Thirty," she repeats, fixing me with a glare.

Just then, I feel a warm body approach

behind me, and a thick, strong hand comes to rest gently on my shoulder. At the same time, the woman's face transforms into a bright smile.

"Grant, honey, how lovely to see you."

"How've you been? How's the farm coming?" the man interjects.

"Great to see you too, Etna," he replies to her first, bobbing his head. "And it's coming along, Hank, slowly but surely. I see you've met my business partner, Sasha."

"Your partner, is it now?" Etna's eyebrows rise.

I remember her now, though. Those names —Etna, Hank—they triggered memories I didn't even know were buried in my head. I remember Mama going over to tea at their place sometimes on Saturdays, when I couldn't have been more than ten years old. I remember cavorting around their yard with some other kids. What were their names? I shake my head. Don't know, but still.

I extend a hand, smiling. "Etna, I'm sorry, I

didn't recognize you at first. How are your kids doing?"

She smiles back, her cheeks flushing a little, clearly surprised and pleased that I remember anything at all. "Just fine, thank you dear. And, a bit belated I suppose, but my sincerest condolences about your mother. She was a fine woman, Maryanne."

"You're the spitting image of her," Hank puts in, a little warmer now that I've spoken up. But still. There's a downturn at the corner of his mouth, a faint suspicion in his gaze. When he glances back at Grant, though, he's all smiles again. "Hope you aren't tiring yourself out too much, working up there all alone."

"Got some help now," Grant says with a smile, his hand tightening slightly on my shoulder.

Just that touch, even through the fabric of my T-shirt, is enough to make my body tense and a pulse of electricity flare in my nerves, deep in my belly.

77

"I hate to say hey and run, but…" Grant gestures from the supplies to the clock above the couple's head. "Running low on sunlight and high on chores, so."

"Of course, no problem, honey." Etna beams. Then she darts a glance at me, something maybe almost apologetic in her gaze, before she turns to start counting up the items. "All together?"

"Sure," Grant says before I can butt in.

I turn to glance at him all too aware of his hand still resting on my shoulder. "Grant," I start in a low voice, but he cuts across me in a voice just as low.

"I'm saving receipts," he says. "They're all business deductions, we'll take it out of the profits once we've sold the place."

"You're selling?" Hank butts in now, eyes wide.

"That's the plan," Grant replies, now looking over my head at the man. But I can't help but notice the tightness around his jaw, or the way his hand drops off my shoulder and he doesn't meet my gaze anymore.

What's that about?

I don't have time to wonder, because Etna's already finished bagging up our supplies, and Grant accepts them from her to lead us out of the store.

I trail after, casting one last glance over my shoulder at the couple to wave as we leave. They wave back, though I have a feeling it's mostly for Grant's sake, from the way their eyes narrow when they catch mine, and their hands drop back to their laps the second Grant is out of sight.

We load up the truck in silence, and I climb into the cab—after Grant yet again insists on opening the door and helping me up—without a word.

"I need to stop at the grocery on the way back," he says. "Figured I'd cook tonight. You want to do a run too?"

"Sure," I mumble.

He lets that sit for a few seconds. "What's eating you?" he asks when he starts the truck up again.

"Nothing." I glance out the window.

He snorts faintly. I spin to glare at him.

"What's so funny?"

"You acting like a grumpy teenager," he replies bluntly. "You don't want to talk about it?"

I bite the inside of my cheek again, annoyed at how easily he can read me. At how transparent I'm being. "It's nothing," I say. "It's just…" I sigh. "The way Etna and Hank were, the way Mark was yesterday… People don't like me here. They don't want me around."

"Why do you care what they think?" Grant replies with a shrug. "You left this place behind for a reason once. You're planning to do the same thing again. What's it matter to you how the people you left behind feel about that?"

He has a point. I lean back in my seat and wrap my hands around the belt, tugging at it. Why *do* I care, anyway? I'm never going to see these people again. I didn't have a damn thing to do with them for fifteen years, not since I left for my better, far more exciting life in the city. Why do I care if they resent me for having that life, for choosing it over this one?

"Fair point," I mumble, not quite sure how to respond. How do I articulate why it bugs me? Because, despite the fact that I *shouldn't* give a damn what anyone in this town thinks… It does still bother me. I just can't put a finger on *why*.

We hit the grocery store, shopping in separate aisles. I finish a lot faster—I figure Grant has a lot to stock up on, since he lives here, whereas I'm just passing through. I only need enough to get me through this week, and in my book, that's mostly pasta and ramen, plus a few fruits and veg for my lunchtime salads.

I check out, but still no sign of him, so I figure I'll get a head start and haul my bags out to the truck before he can come and offer to carry everything for me again, Country Man With Manners style.

I get my bags situated in the truck bed which he's left unlocked—*I'm going to have to get used to that again*, I think for a second before I remember that no, I don't have to get used to it at all, since I'll be leaving for the big city again in just a few more days. As I'm about to climb into the truck, a shout stalls me.

"Sasha?" a guy hollers.

There's a whistle as I stop and turn around slowly.

"It *is*," the guy says again. I don't recognize him. "Sasha Bluebell in the flesh." He's across the street, but when I make eye contact, he steps off the curb and starts strolling toward me. "Damn. You've filled out." His gaze drops across my body. Unlike when Grant does that, this feels sleazy. Irritating as hell, especially when he licks his lips after.

I don't remember him, but that's clearly becoming a running theme. "Excuse me. You are?" I ask, planting my hands on my hips.

Unlike most people who seem annoyed or

irritated when I don't recognize them, this guy's smirk only deepens. "Aaron Smith. You don't remember me? We went to junior high together. Though…" He shakes his head with another grin— and another long, lingering look at my body, which makes me cross my arms across my stomach and glare. He's still walking closer. Just a foot away now. "You definitely looked a lot different back then. Fair enough. Bet I did too."

You probably weren't a scrawny creeper with greasy hair and a lecher's grin, I think. Then again, what do I know. "Aaron. Nice to see you. Afraid I was just leaving." I grab the handle of the passenger side door.

He grabs my hand, pins it against the handle. "Aw. You leaving so fast? You only just got back into town from what I hear."

"Yeah, well, never was my favorite place," I manage to growl between clenched teeth. "This is reminding me why."

His eyes darken. "What's the matter, Sasha?

Too good for us country boys now?" He leans in, and I catch a whiff of something horrible on his breath. Rotten egg scent. "Or do you just need a good roll in the hay as a reminder of how good we can be?" he asks with a wink.

My stomach churns. I wrench my hand free of his and open my mouth to let him have it.

But before I can, a deeper, angrier voice interrupts. "Leave her alone."

Grant.

Aaron's gaze darts over my head, and he drops his hand. Though he doesn't back off. "What's the matter, bored of the local fare, Werther? Got a taste for fancier gals now?"

"None of your fucking business, Smith," he replies. Unlike Aaron, his tone isn't antagonistic or angry. Grant doesn't need to threaten anyone to be intimidating, I realize. He just... *is*.

"No need to snap. I wasn't criticizing your taste." Aaron winks again. "Big city girl is a looker, if not a keeper."

84

"You know what's also none of your fucking business, Smith?" Grant asks. I turn to find him smiling serenely. Utterly unconcerned. Only his eyes give him away. There's a red-hot fire burning in them. It's the kind of glare no sane person would fuck with. "Ms. Bluebell. Who, by the way, is a person, and not the inanimate object you're making her sound like right now." His lip turns up, his nose lifting in a faint sneer of disdain. "Though with guys like you chasing her around this town, I'd hardly say anyone can blame her for high-tailing it out of here first chance she got."

My eyes widen, even as my heart beats faster. *Fuck.* No guy has ever defended me like that before.

Aaron, for his part, is scowling now. But even he seems to know better than to fuck with Grant. He's about a third of Grant's size and doesn't look like he's got any muscle to speak of either. "Fuck you too, Werther," he mutters as he turns away.

"Great to see you as always," Grant calls at his back, rolling his eyes and storming past me to toss his groceries in the truck. "Little fucker's begging to get his ass wiped across this street if you ask me," he mutters as he swings back around to open my door for me. He locks eyes with me for a second, something apologetic there. "Do me one favor. Don't judge us all by that rotten shit-shaped apple."

"I don't," I answer without thinking. I can't tear my eyes from his. Can't stop my heart racing either, at the thought of the way he just defended me without even so much as lifting a finger. Though I know he would—I know he'd have kicked Aaron's ass if he had to in my defense.

That only makes it even hotter.

There's a long, tense moment as we stand there, breathing the same air, my head tilted back so I can stare up at him fully.

Then Grant pulls away, strides back around to the driver's side of the truck without waiting for me to climb in and shut the door behind me like usual.

I pull myself into the cabin and try to ignore the way my fingertips quiver; my hands shake as I buckle myself into the seat.

We take the drive back toward the farm in silence. I chew on the inside of my cheek, not sure how to break it. When we finally make the turn up the dirt road toward the farm itself, I take a deep breath and force the words out.

"Thank you," I say. "For defending me."

"I'd defend anyone from that asshole," he replies. "Aaron Smith hasn't been worth a damn since the second his poor mother was unfortunate enough to squat him out."

I laugh softly and shake my head. "Still," I continue. "I... Thanks."

We drive up the dirt road in bumping silence for a while. I glance back down at my jeans—the same jeans that my ass showed in earlier this morning. The jeans that I traipsed around town in after Grant. No wonder Aaron tried to pull something.

I shake my head. "I should be more careful, probably."

He glances sideways at me without responding, then guns it a little faster. The house pulls into sight up the road.

"I mean…" I tug at my jeans. "Like, with my outfits and everything. I should be more careful about drawing attention to myself…"

Grant doesn't answer until we pull into a parking spot next to the cabin. When he puts the car into park, he turns to cast a long look at me, gaze dropping to my jeans and then back to my face. "You're right," he says, reaching to undo his own belt.

I blink. "What…"

"You shouldn't draw attention to yourself," he speaks over me, faster, sounding frustrated now. Maybe even angry.

I frown.

"Drawing attention to yourself could cause trouble you never expected. More than you asked for." His dark eyes catch mine, and there's something white hot in them now. My belly clenches, even as my pussy responds by going tighter, feeling wet. "Drawing attention to yourself could make it really hard for a man like me to avoid bending your sexy ass over and fucking you right here in the dirt."

My mouth drops open. It takes a second for me to find my voice. When I do, I have to take a deep breath to keep it from trembling with desire. "You're... being too forward, Mr. Werther."

He barks out a laugh at that, so sharp and close that it makes me jump in my seat slightly. "*Mr. Werther.* I think we're past that now, Sasha. Or was that not you I caught this afternoon, sneaking around the house stealing peeks at my big dick in the shower?"

My cheeks flare red-hot. *Fuck.* He saw that?

He grins, as though to answer my internal

question. "Tell me, did you like what you saw? You certainly hung around looking for long enough."

Unbidden, unable to help myself, my gaze drops to his lap again now. There's a bulge in his jeans, though judging by his size earlier, it's hard to tell if he's already hard for me or if that's just how fucking big he is, even when he's not hard yet. "I…"

"Or were you nervous?" He raises an eyebrow, studying me. "Scared of the big country man and his huge cock. Huh, Sasha?"

I can't do this. I can't stay here or I'm going to say—or do—something I fucking regret. I grab my handle and fling the door open. Throw myself down from the passenger seat and ball up my fists. I try to think of a retort, something to shout. But he's right. I *did* sneak around watching him shower. I can't exactly call him out for being crude now.

Especially not when my pussy is wetter than it's been in months at hearing him say all that. Hearing him talk about fucking me in the dirt, about how big his cock is…

So I just turn my back and storm up toward the house.

There's a slam as Grant shuts his own door. "That's right," he calls across the yard. "Scared little city girl. Run on home to the big city before you get hurt out here in the real world."

I growl under my breath as I reach the front door. I fling it open with a crash and stomp inside, furious. I slam it behind me again, hard enough that the frame creaks in protest. I ignore it and stomp right through the house, grabbing the tool bag on the way through. *Damn.* I left the nails I need to finish the roof back in the truck.

Doesn't matter. I'll work on something else in the meantime. Anything to get me out of this house and away from that asshole.

Drawing attention to yourself could make it hard to avoid bending your sexy ass over and fucking you.

I shiver. Dammit. Why are my panties so

fucking wet at the thought of that? What kind of asshole talks like that to his business partner?

That's what we are after all. That's *all* we are here. Business partners, trying to be professional while fixing up this hellhole and selling it to the highest bidder. He has no right to assume anything about me, to talk about fucking me, just because…

Just because you perved on him in the shower?

I grimace. All I did was peek a little. I was curious. So sue me. But he's way out of line.

That's what I tell myself, anyway, as I hole up next to the rosebush that's taken over the tool shed out back and start to work trimming away the weeds that have interwoven between the thorny branches. If I don't trim this thing back, it'll take down the walls of this shed in a summer or two. So I sink myself into my repair work, and do my best to ignore any thoughts about the asshole I left standing beside his stupid truck.

Chapter 5

Grant Werther

Fuck. I probably took that too far. But what the hell was I supposed to say with her sitting right there in my truck smelling the way she does, so fucking intoxicating, and dressed in those barely-there booty shorts that make me hard just looking at her.

It was hard enough shopping today without getting so hard I'd draw stares from every mile around. I had to keep avoiding her in the hardware store and again at the grocery, because the way her sexy, tight little ass played peekaboo in those jean shorts made me think about how tight she'd be if I bent her over the backseat of my truck and thrust my thick dick inside her wet little pussy…

Fuck. There I go again.

Dammit, Sasha. She drives me insane. No matter how much I try not to think about her, I can't stop.

Probably because she's always right there in front of me, wearing some sexy, skimpy little shorts, bending over and flashing that pert, perfect ass of hers, or pouting in that way she has when she's debating which tile she wants to lay where...

Damn. Here I go again.

I clench my fists. I'll jerk one out in the shower later—the same way I've been aching to ever since I caught her peering through the shower door at me, trying to catch a glimpse of my dick. Seems like she caught a peek of more than she bargained for, to judge by the way she ran inside after I called her out in the truck.

Well, good. She should run. I'm more than she can handle. In more ways than one. Size-wise, country-man-wise, hell, just every way. She's not ready for a wild man. She likes tame, placid little city boys.

She should run back to those boys before she winds up getting hurt. Before I wind up hurting her. Because I would. A city girl like her, god, the things I could do to her... She'd be in way over her head, and she'd lose her head, and then where would she be left? Pining for a country man who she never wants to see again, because just like this whole town, Sasha Bluebell has always been too damn good for me.

I shake my head and finish hauling the last load of groceries and hardware supplies inside. Out back, through the little window over the kitchen sink, I spot Sasha out by the shed. She's abandoned the roofing for now, probably because I still have all the nails she needs in here, and she's clearly not ready to be in the same room as me for a while, let alone talk to me.

But she's still working, I'll give her that. City Girl has some backbone after all. Not to mention some work ethic.

For a moment I hesitate at the sink, just watching her reach up to yank down the stray vines growing in and between the rose bushes. She's cutting back some of the roses too, but in a careful way, shows she knows what she's doing. I'm surprised. I didn't think that girl had any of her Mama in her—only her runaway Daddy. But watching her now, I can see the Maryanne my Pops was best friends with. The woman who owned and ran this whole farm by herself, without asking anyone for help. Even when Pops bailed her out of the hole she wound up in after a few too many crop blights, Maryanne was proud. She swore she'd buy the other half of the farm back off him one day.

She'd have done it too, I have no doubt, if the cancer didn't get her first. Scary how diseases like that creep up on you. One minute she's hale as an ox, and scary as one to boot. Ready to take on Pops, me, hell, half the town if she had a mind to. Everyone hereabouts loved her—it's part of the reason people blamed her daughter so much for running off and leaving her alone. But you catch Maryanne letting anyone in this town say one bad word about her baby Sasha in earshot, and you'd have had yourself a real fireworks display. Maryanne didn't stand for any of that. She was proud of her daughter.

My chest aches watching Sasha now. I shake my head and ignore it.

Sasha isn't her mama. That much is clear from her attitude, her city-slicker outfits, her fancy car, those ridiculous damn high heels she wore yesterday. At least she abandoned those today, thank Christ.

But Sasha is getting more and more interesting to me nevertheless. Not least because just now, as I'm watching over the kitchen sink, she yanks a whole branch of crawling vine free and bends over to stuff it into the garbage bag she's working with.

Which provides me with a picture-perfect view of that ass, the bottoms of her cheeks peeking out the bottoms of her short, short little jeans.

Fuck.

I can feel my cock digging into the kitchen

cabinets, I'm so hard.

Unable to resist, I slide a hand down to my zipper.

I shouldn't. Especially not *here*. But Sasha is busy with her work. She tosses her head, long blonde curls flying, and fuck, what I wouldn't give to have those curls wrapped around my fist. To pull them tight and watch her neck arch, her perfect cupid's bow lips parting with a loud cry as I buried my cock inside her tight pussy.

I unzip my fucking jeans.

She keeps working, oblivious to the man in the kitchen.

But it's only fair, I think. She peeped on me in the shower. She stood there for at least a minute while I rinsed off the soap, keeping my cock in her view all the while because I knew what she came for, and to be honest, it turned me on to see her watching. But she started this.

Besides, she's not even naked right now.

Fuck, imagine her naked.

My cock is so hard that by the time I pull it out of my boxers, it's practically jumping in my fist. I wrap my fist around the base and start to pump along my shaft, slowly, imagining taking Sasha by the hips right now. Pushing her down onto her hands and knees in the dirt where she's working. Bending her over that bag she's stuffing with leaves and weeds. Yanking those ridiculous excuses for shorts down until they puddled around her knees. Pushing aside whatever skimpy underwear she has on and positioning my big, thick cock right at the entrance to her soaking wet pussy.

I'd make her beg first. Oh, yes. I'd make her scream for me. Tell me how much she wants me. Beg me to fuck her until she can't walk straight.

Only then would I finally push the tip of my thick cock between her lips. Slide inch by inch into her pussy, and enjoy the way she moaned and groaned as her tight walls expanded to take me.

I stroke myself faster, faster. It's almost embarrassing how fast I near the edge, how I have to back off and move my hand slower for a while, think about running my hands over her ass and digging one hand into that luscious long hair, in order to stave off the peak from hitting too soon.

Finally, though, I can't hold it off any longer. I grab a wad of paper towels from the sink and come into them with a groan, teeth gritted, eyes still fixed on the window, on Sasha.

She's working away, completely oblivious. She has no idea the kind of effect she has on men.

On *me*.

I shake my head and sigh. I'd have thought that would satiate me somewhat. But I only feel more riled up than ever now. I want that girl something fierce. But damned if I'm going to take her. Not with all this mess going on.

Don't mix business and pleasure, I remind myself as I finish cleaning up and toss away the evidence. I cast one last glance at the window before I go to behave. To finish my chores for the day and head back out to sleep in the bed of my truck for another night.

But that's when I freeze.

Because this time when I look outside, Sasha isn't working.

She's turned sideways. For a moment I think she must have lost something. She's bent double, hands on her head.

Then she sags forward, onto her knees, and I fling myself at the door. *Something's wrong.*

I sprint out back, door crashing behind me. I'm already on the lawn by the time she drops to all fours.

"Sasha!"

She doesn't respond. From the way she's bent though, head almost touching the dirt, it can't be good.

I reach her side in a few seconds, and breathe a sigh of relief when she turns her head, at least far enough to study my shoes.

"I…" She shakes her head, probably smearing dirt across her forehead, since it's still pressed against the ground.

"Come here." I bend and scoop her up easily, all in one motion. Christ, the girl weighs almost nothing. When was the last time she had a decent meal?

Now I sound like a damn grandmother. What is this woman doing to me?

"What happened?" I ask, cradling her against my chest. "Look at me, Sasha."

Her head is swaying, and when she does look up, her eyes are unfocused, sliding across my face before she zeroes in on my eyes and blinks.

"I... don't know..."

"Do you feel dizzy? Lightheaded? Describe the symptoms to me."

"I... Yeah, dizzy," she admits.

I'm already striding toward the house, carrying her as fast as my legs will move. "Have you eaten something today? Drank any water?"

"Um..." She bites her lip. "Breakfast. And..."

"When was the last time you had water?" I prompt.

"I… don't know."

I heave a sigh. "You need to stay hydrated if you're going to spend all day out in the sun playing at farmhand, City Girl."

A small smile tugs at the corner of her lips at that nickname. Good. Smiling is good. Understanding jokes is good. "My bad. Forgot… We don't have… Water in the city."

I laugh at that even as I shoulder our way through the back door.

When we get inside the house, she swings her legs a little. "I can stand…"

"No way." I breeze right through the kitchen, bypassing the living room, which only has a couple of armchairs, not anything you can really lie down on. I carry her straight into the bedroom and lay her down on the bed, taking care not to jostle her too much on the way down.

"Really, I'm fine," she protests as soon as

I've got her lying flat. She tries to sit up but I can tell from the way that her eyes slide in and out of focus that she's bullshitting me.

"You're not fine." I catch her shoulders and gently press her back down onto the bed. "Promise me you won't try to sit up while I get you water."

She heaves a sigh but catches my eye, and something in my look must tell her I'm serious. "I promise," she accedes.

Only then do I slip out of the room to go and fill her a huge glass of water. When I get back, my shoulders relax a little, seeing that she's still awake, alert, and not trying to sit up or push me on this anymore. I sit on the edge of the bed and slide a hand between her shoulder blades—ignoring the pang that this intimate contact sends straight to my groin. *It's not the time.*

I hold her upright, just far enough to drink. She takes a huge gulp at first, but I pull the cup away from her lip. "Small sips," I say. "At least until the first wave of dizziness passes."

She takes a couple of sips, then I help her lie back down and set the glass on the nightstand. Sasha heaves another sigh, this one the type of sigh I recognize. She's frustrated.

"I was trying to help," she says, her voice small, annoyed with herself. "I can work, you know. I'm not some completely spoiled brat."

"I know that." I'm standing again, because I don't trust myself lingering here next to her for too long. If I hang around and watch her lying across this bed, it won't be long before I start picturing other ways the two of us could sprawl across it. And that will only lead to trouble.

Trouble for her.

And probably for me too, since then I'll have fucked my business partner.

"You need to be careful," I tell her. "Take care of yourself. Don't push too hard. Even if you can work, your body isn't used to this pace."

She nods a little, mouth pursed.

I glance past her at the window. "Catch

some rest," I tell her. "It's getting late anyway. I'll finish the roof, then make us some dinner. Sound good?"

She bites her lip. "You don't have to take care of me."

"I know," I reply. I'm out of the room before she can say anything else.

I don't have to. Doesn't mean I won't, at least when she's like this.

City Girl is in way over her head here.

Chapter 6

Sasha Bluebell

How fucking embarrassing. First I go and faint in front of Grant. Then he forces me to let him carry me inside and take care of me…

But I can't lie, he's good at it. Not to mention how good it felt being cradled in his arms —at least once I was awake enough to realize what was happening, to feel his strong arms holding me against his rock-solid chest, and feel his breath on my cheeks as he leaned down to check on me, asking me questions, cracking jokes to check if I was still awake and with-it.

And when he helped me sit up to drink water, his touch against my back felt red-hot, almost as distracting as the itch in my throat and the pounding, dizzying ache in my head from the dehydration.

Now, he's cooked a veritable feast, which

he's forcing me to eat in bed like I'm an invalid.

"I can sit at the table," I protest.

"That would ruin the whole point of dinner-in-bed," he replies with a shrug as he sets the tray across my lap. The breakfast-in-bed tray. I remember this. We used to bring it in to Mama every Mother's Day, serve her pancakes on it.

We?

No. I used to. I used to, every year after my good-for-nothing father left us to fend for ourselves on Mother's Day and every other day of the year.

I force that thought to the back of my mind. *Don't think about it*. Like always. Like I've been doing for years.

I smile a little half-smile at Grant, and glance from him to the feast. He grilled corn and potatoes the same way Mama used to, baking them in tinfoil, then searing them a bit at the end so they're black and flaky around the edges, not to mention coated in plenty of salt. His ribs look a hell of a lot better than any Mama ever made though, and covered in BBQ sauce. All that combined with the fat slices of bread and the veritable vat of butter he included, and, well...

"This looks like the worst possible thing we could eat in bed," I point out with a laugh, eying the single handful of napkins he brought with it dubiously.

"Why, are you a messy eater, Sasha?" He lifts an eyebrow, smirking at me.

"Depends what I'm eating," I say, before I realize. I blush a little and roll my eyes as he snorts with laughter. "I meant *like ribs*, which are going to get all over my hands and my face."

"Uh huh. That the only thing you like all over your hands and face?" He raises a single eyebrow, pinning me with his stare.

I remember what he said in the car. The way he thinks about me. Not going to lie, the whole time I was out working in the yard, the memory of that comment kept me more than a little worked up.

As annoyed as I might be by him making

that comment, threatening to make this relationship anything but a business one, I have to admit… It's hot as hell to know that I'm just as distracting to Grant Werther as he is to me. The big country man might be a danger to the little city girl, but apparently, he's not immune to my charms either.

Which is good to know.

So I grab a rib and take a bite, catching his eye while I chew it, then lick the BBQ sauce slowly off my lips. "Course not," I reply. "Who doesn't like to get good and messy once in a while?"

His grin widens. But the way his eyes go dark and hungry, that he can't disguise. Oh yeah. Grant fucking wants me. And wants to fuck me, for sure.

I want to fuck him too.

Damn.

We're treading on thin ice here. But there's something about being this reckless that's a relief, after all the dates I've been on in the city lately. Those are all dancing around the point, beating around the bush until my bush gets so tired of all the double-talk that I just give up and go to bed. At least Grant is direct. At least with him, I know exactly how much trouble I'm getting into because he tells me straight upfront.

I finish off that rib while he takes one of his own, then lay it down on the plate and reach for a napkin. On second thought, though, I pause and raise a finger to my lips. I lick the BBQ sauce off slowly, eyes locked on his, and grin as he narrows his eyes.

"But don't get any sauce on these sheets," I say. "We've only got one bed, you know."

"*You've* only got one bed," he points out. "Me, I've got a whole truck bed to myself. That one I don't mind getting dirty either."

My cheeks flush. "We can trade," I say. "I'll take my car tonight. It's only fair."

He snorts. "What kind of a gentleman would I be if I let the lady who nearly passed out from dehydration and exhaustion in the yard today sleep in her damn car when there's a perfectly good bed right here."

"Well, if you can manage not to dirty up the bed with dinner, we could..." I pause. Swallow that last word.

He raises an eyebrow. Doesn't say anything. Doesn't prompt me, but doesn't change the subject, either.

I shake my head. "Just, sleep wherever tonight. It doesn't bother me." That said, I grab another rib and stuff it into my mouth before I say something I'll really regret. Something like *sleep with me in this bed tonight—and for the love of God, please do more than just sleep here.*

Or something more his style, more direct. Something like *Please fuck me right here in the middle of this delicious tray of BBQ you just cooked.*

If there's one thing sexier than a big, sexy country man who takes care of you when you're sick, it's a big sexy country man who takes care of you and knows how to cook a mean rib. I've tried grilling ribs for my friends back in the city about a million times, but none of them ever turn out right. None of them ever taste quite like home.

I'd almost forgotten what real ribs taste like, until these.

Grant, for his part, lets up on the flirting long enough to finish eating, at least. I'm still licking my fingers when he grabs the tray to whisk it off.

"Non-cook does dishes," I call after him.

He just shouts back from the kitchen, "Lie back down."

I groan and collapse back onto the pillows. "I'm not an invalid," I protest. But protests aside, it doesn't take long for my eyelids to droop. I manage to drag myself out of bed long enough to wash my face and brush my teeth, then I slink back into the room and slip under the covers. I'm out before I even remember to turn off the light.

Farming is hard work.

I wake up to a faint motion. I squint at the ceiling—the light is off now. It takes me a moment, in the moonlit farmhouse, to remember where exactly I am. It takes me even longer to realize what the faint sigh beside me means, and to recognize the presence of another warm body.

I roll over, eyes widening, to find Grant sound asleep next to me. He's on his back, face turned away from me, but he's fast asleep, chest rising and falling in a slow, steady rhythm.

He's shirtless too. Only his boxers on, which I can tell because he's lying on top of the covers instead of underneath, heat practically radiating off his body. Normally I'm cold at night, especially in this little farmhouse on the brink of fall without any indoor heating besides the wood stove in the kitchen to go by. But the room feels hot with Grant here, and not just temperature-wise.

I sit up a little. "Grant?" I whisper, softly, just to check.

Nothing. No reaction. I lie back down and

continue to watch him, a flush spreading over my cheeks.

He's fucking hot as hell.

He sighs softly and rolls over, away from me. I sit up a little, checking whether he's woken up. But no. He's still sound asleep. With his face relaxed in sleep, he's even more attractive. His cheekbones stand out sharply in the moonlight, and his eyelids flutter faintly. Dreaming, I'd guess, from the way his fingertips twitch and his hips shift a little.

I trace my eyes down his bare chest, along the stark ridges of his muscles, and then I draw in a sharp breath.

Definitely dreaming. And something very, very enjoyable to judge by the way his cock stands at attention, rock hard, the big, thick outline visible even through his boxers. Tent is putting it mildly— he's building a whole fort down there.

It doesn't take much imagination to picture what's under that thin fabric. I saw how big he was even when he wasn't hard in the shower. Now, he looks like he's got one of those novelty-store dildos in his pants, the ones that are so big you wonder if anyone could possibly have a dick that size.

What would that feel like inside me?

He'd hurt, probably, at least at first. But fuck, how good would it feel once we got going? How hard would this big country man fuck me if I let him?

Is that what he's dreaming about right now? He talked about wanting to bend me over and fuck me in the dirt... Is he picturing doing that to me now as he sleeps? Picturing us out in the field, him tearing off my skimpy little jean shorts and stuffing that fat cock inside me?

I slide my hand down the flat plane of my stomach, toward my PJ shorts. I wore them to be decent, same with the little sleep tank top. Now I'm wishing I'd gone a bit bolder. Thong and a lace bra, maybe, or even less. Clearly Grant would've appreciated it.

Fuck. I shouldn't do this. He might wake up at any moment. But I can't help myself. Between his words earlier and how frustrated I got myself this afternoon, working out in the fields trying—and failing—not to think about how hard he'd fuck me, how good it would feel. Between that and his ministrations later, after I got sick, and how fucking sexy he looks all the damn time, and how he defended me in town when that Aaron creep came onto me…

I can't help myself. He's lying right here next to me having a dirty fantasy of his own, and I can't help picturing the same thing.

I slip my hand under the hem of my shorts. Straight down the front of my tight little panties.

Fuck. I'm already wet.

I part my lips with two fingers, tracing the edges of my pussy. I imagine this is Grant's hand, Grant touching me, feeling me, exploring. *Scared of the big country man and his huge cock?* His voice echoes in my mind. That cocksure grin of his. He's

Trouble with a capital T, and I know it.

That only makes me want him all the more.

He'd spread my legs and lean down along my body, that rough beard of his scratching my belly as he licked and sucked and bit his way down from my bellybutton, all the way to my mound. I swirl my fingers across my mound, my lips, grazing my clit and stifling a faint gasp as I do. I picture him yanking my panties down, grinning up at me before he leans down to kiss my pussy lips, one at a time, then running his tongue along them, slow, teasing.

He'd want to work me up first. He'd have to, to get me ready to take that big cock of his.

I press my fingers between my pussy lips, imagining his thick, rough fingers there instead. I push two fingers into my pussy at once, to imitate his thick girth. But his fingers would be even thicker, rougher. He'd waste no time curling them against my inner wall, going right for the G-spot, because he doesn't fuck around. I imagine the hungry look in his eyes from earlier, the way he'd stare up at me as he finger-fucked me, slowly at first, then building up momentum.

I imagine this, and I shift in the bed, eyes still focused on his sexy half-naked body, his sharp muscles, the curve of his jaw, the size of his hands. I reach out and curl my free hand in the sheets just inches from his, feeling the blaze of his warmth against my skin, even with a few inches of bed still between my hand and his.

I imagine those fingers inside me, even as I stroke myself faster, bring myself closer to climax. I've been able to stay quiet so far, but as I near my peak, it gets harder. My mouth falls open and my hips buck a little, as hard as I try to keep them still. I inhale sharply, still stroking, faster, faster, so close to the edge, so close... I can't quite help the soft gasp that escapes me.

At that sound, Grant rolls over to face me.

I startle and pull my fingers out of my pussy. But his eyes are wide open, and my hand is still down the front of my pants, and he's smirking at me, one eyebrow raised.

"Don't stop on my account," he says, his voice low and sexy as fuck, even though the sound is startling in the otherwise silent room.

"I…" I bite my lip and slide my hand out of my pants, trying to wipe my fingers along the sheets. "It's not…"

"You must be so close now." Grant shifts closer. There's barely an inch of space between us. We're nose-to-nose, almost touching. His eyes bore into mine. "It's got to ache to stop when you're that close."

"I wasn't…" I swallow hard and blink, unable to deny it. Unable to confirm it either. I'm stunned, pinned in place by those dark blazing eyes of his.

Without warning, he reaches down and cups me. I gasp, the warm, strong heat of his hands so much hotter than I imagined. Like everything else about him, his hands are *big*. And warm, and rough…

He squeezes a little tighter, his fingers pressing against my pussy through the fabric of my shorts and my panties. I can feel the damp even through both layers, and so can he, to judge by the smirk on his face. "Isn't it driving you wild, Sasha?" He rotates his palm a little, grinding it against my mound, and I buck up into him with a moan, unable to help myself.

With his other hand, he catches my free hand, the one I'd been using to touch myself. He lifts it to his lips, trails the flat blade of his tongue across my fingers, and groans slightly with pleasure, his eyes fluttering closed. "Fuck, you taste as good as you smell," he murmurs.

My pussy pulses at the sound of that.

He draws my hand down his body, brings it to rest against the hard head of his cock. I glance down, eyes widening. My hand doesn't even fit around him. I wrap my palm around the head of his cock, trail my hand down his side slowly, tracing his length slowly, up and down. As I do, he reaches up and pushes my shorts down, followed by my panties just after. I gasp as the cool evening air hits my pussy. But he doesn't leave me exposed for long. His palm clamps back across my mound, red hot, and his fingers spread my lower lips, tracing my lips one at a time with slow, teasing strokes.

I imitate him, push his boxers down to fully expose his cock, but even prepared as I think I am, having seen him before and touched him just now, I still gasp when he springs free. His cock is fucking huge. The veins bulge along the sides of his shaft, and the swollen head of his cock pulses with lust. There's a bead of precum gathered at his tip already and I trace my thumb across it, trail it back down the underside of his cock, tracing the vein there.

"You like what you see?" Grant smirks, knowing. "You like my big fucking cock, City Girl?"

I swallow hard, eyes still focused on his length, his width. "Fuck yes," I whisper.

"You think you can handle me? Think your tight little city pussy can take it? Because I don't know…" He grins, and with that, pushes one finger inside me.

My whole body arcs up off the bed. I gasp aloud, arching into his hand, and my clit digs into the heel of his palm as I do, only doubling the sensation. His finger feels so thick inside me, twisting as he runs it along my inner walls, a different one with every stroke as he begins to push it in and out of me. "You feel pretty tight to me, City Girl."

"Maybe," I admit, my voice low, breathless. "But I'm wet for you too…" I buck up into him, stifling a groan as the motion forces his finger deeper into me.

He crooks his finger, drags it along my front inner wall until his fingertip finds the hard, sensitive graze of my G-spot. Then he works back and forth along that, even as I tighten my fist on his cock and reach up with my other hand, using both now to

123

pump along his length harder.

"You think that'll be enough?" He smirks. "Let's see if we can't get you even wetter…" He strokes faster, and I moan aloud. Then he adds a second finger, and my pussy tightens, tenses around the width of his fingers. With his thumb, he grazes my clit, over and over with each stroke, hitting my G-spot and the edges of my clit at once. The sensations threaten to send me over the edge, but I tighten my grip on his cock and fuck him faster, not ready to give in yet.

I'm rewarded by a faint groan, deep in the back of his throat, as his eyes go hooded and feral with lust.

"You like that?" I whisper, grinning.

In response, he rolls over, positioned on his knees above me, and continues to finger me hard, fast. I keep fisting his cock, with it aimed right at my chest now, using both hands, my eyes on his balls as they swing beneath him.

Fuck, I want to take him into my mouth. I

want to suck him until he's about to come, and then let him come all over my chest, my mouth. I want to taste him, feel him, make him lose control.

But his fingers are too distracting, and his body, arched up like this above mine, tears away too much of my attention. Before long my hips are bucking against the bed of their own accord, and my mouth falls open, my head twisting against the sheets as I moan and writhe under him.

"That's right, you're close now aren't you, Sasha? Fucking come for me, City Girl. Come on my fingers."

I gasp and arch up against him. He curls two fingers inside me, presses his thumb over my clit and thrusts those fingers in, once, twice…

I can't stave it off any longer. I cry out, my voice shaky, as the orgasm hits me. It tears through my nerves, sets my veins on fire, and my whole body bucks along the bed with the force of it.

"That's right, come hard City Girl. Keep coming." Grant, for his part, doesn't stop stroking me. Even when my hands fall away from his cock so I can twist them in the sheets, lost in pleasure. He keeps fingering me until I fall back against the sheets, panting, my body sheened with sweat.

He draws his fingers out of me with a faint pop, and I feel the slick of my own juices along my inner thigh. He leans back, sitting on his heels as he watches me, a satisfied smile on his face, even though his eyes are still dark with want.

"Now there's the orgasm you so desperately needed," he comments, smirking. "You were so thirsty for it you couldn't help touching yourself right next to me, huh? Didn't listen before when I told you you were courting trouble."

I swallow hard, but reach for his hands. Grab them and pull him down until he's leaning over me on all fours. "I still want trouble," I tell him, eyes locked on his.

"Good," he replies without missing a beat. "Because at this point, Sasha, I can't help but fuck you. You've driven me too fucking wild for too fucking long."

I lick my lips. Trace my eyes down his chest. Straight to that thick cock of his, stiff and hard as ever, pointing so low between his legs now that it makes my eyes widen.

"Yeah," he says, following my gaze. "That's the problem, though. I still doubt your city pussy can handle my big country cock."

I lift my chin, stubborn, and lock eyes with him. "I was born and raised here same as you, Grant Werther," I point out. "I think I can handle what you've got to give."

He laughs, low and throaty, in a dangerous way that makes my belly tighten. But he bows his head, eyes locked onto mine, nevertheless. "Fair enough then. Let's find out how you take it."

With that, he grabs both of my ankles at once and pulls me down the bed, flat onto my back beneath him. He kneels between my thighs and I wrap my legs around his waist, arching up until my pussy is pointed right at the tip of his cock.

"I've waited too long for this," he murmurs, his voice a low, possessive growl as he lowers himself toward me, positions the tip of his cock at my entrance.

I clamp my mouth shut to avoid moaning, but when he pushes the tip of his cock between my lips, his head slowly penetrating my pussy, I can't help it. My mouth falls open and I moan aloud at the sensation.

He takes it slow, steady, pushing himself into me a centimeter at a time, letting my pussy stretch and adjust to his girth slowly. I groan as he keeps going, the stretching, tightening sensation driving me wild. It hurts, but it feels fucking amazing too, to be stuffed so fully, have someone so huge inside me. With every inch deeper he goes, my muscles tense and release, tense and release.

When he's finally buried fully inside me, I reach up to grab his shoulders, running my hands down his back, along the sharp curves of his muscles as he lies along me for a moment, letting me adjust.

He's breathing hard too, a catch in his throat. "Fuck," he groans softly beside my ear, his voice sending another thrill through my nervous system and making my pussy clench—which in turn makes his thick cock jump inside me. "You are so fucking tight it's unbelievable."

With that, he leans back and starts to draw out of me again, and I cry out once more, already missing the feeling of his thick cock deep in me, filling me up. He only pulls out an inch though, before he rocks back in, slow at first, steady, letting me adjust to him.

I buck my hips up against him, but he drops his hands to my hips and pins me flat against the bed.

"You think you can take this?" he murmurs, grinning. He pulls back again, two inches this time, and drives into me once more, a little faster this time, a little harder.

"Fuck yes," I pant. "Give it to me."

"You want me to really fuck you, Sasha?"

"Yes, Grant. I want you to fuck me with your big cock."

He smirks. "How hard do you want me to fuck you?" He pulls back again, teasing, three inches this time. Then he drives into me once more, fast enough to make me gasp.

"Hard," I hiss through clenched teeth, distracted by pleasure.

"How hard?"

"Fucking hard. I want you to fuck me until I can't walk straight. I want you to fuck me so hard it hurts."

His grin widens, and that animal lust in his eyes goes darker, wild. "I underestimated you, City Girl."

"I told you," I manage to pant, also grinning, and I'm sure the look in my eyes right now is just as hungry. "I'm just as country as you, big man. So fuck me like I am."

He pulls all the way out of my pussy, then

drives back into me, his full length now. I scream and dig my nails into his back, pleasure and pain tearing through me in equal measure. He cups my ass with both his big, rough hands and lifts my hips off the bed, holds me in the air between his legs as he starts to fuck me fully, though still slow at first, his hard shaft stretching my pussy, stuffing me whole.

I grip his shoulders with my hands, nails out, and tighten my thighs around his waist. With every thrust, he makes me cry out louder, makes my body ache for release.

I glance down to see his cock thrusting in and out of me, and feel the slap of his balls against my ass cheeks with every fuck. The sensation is unlike anything I've ever felt before. We've pushed straight through any pain there was before—it's all pleasure now. The feeling of being completely full, stuffed so full I can barely take it. The walls of my pussy ache where they strain to hold his thick cock, and it drives me wild.

He picks up the pace, lifting my whole lower half off the bed now, and I arch my hips with him, thrusting against him. His cock drags against my inner walls and I groan every time his head grazes past my G-spot, the pressure mounting so high it makes my pulse beat at the edges of my vision.

"You like that, Sasha?" he pants through a hard smile, his eyes still full of that same hunger, that same lust.

"Fuck yes." I grind my hips up against his as he pounds into me, moving faster now, harder. It drives me wild, after so much build-up, so much unreleased tension.

"You want more?" His voice is a growl, barely contained. He's holding back, I can tell. But I don't want him to. I want to see what this Country Man is made of.

"Fuck yes," I repeat, my own voice a growl too. "Give it to me, Country Man. Fuck me as hard as you can."

He speeds up, fucking me harder, faster. I'm stretched out wide enough to take him now, and it doesn't hurt at all—it only drives me more wild as his thick cock fills every inch of me completely.

It doesn't take long before I'm nearing the brink, my breath coming hard and fast, my hips bucking in time with his.

"You want to come for me?" he asks, low and fast. "You want to come on my big cock?"

"Make me come, Grant. Make me come with your cock."

He leans back and unhooks my legs from around his waist. Flings them over his shoulders to angle his thrusts so the head of his cock drags down the front inner wall of my pussy. I cry aloud at that, unable to stop my body from twisting against the sheets. I lose my grip on his shoulders and fist the sheets instead, trying to thrust back against him. But all I can manage to do is hang on as that fat cock of his drives me straight up to the brink of orgasm.

When it hits me, I scream so loud it would

wake half the neighbors if I were back in New York City. But I'm not in the city—I'm in the country, getting fucked like I've never been fucked before, and out here, there's no one to hear me for miles.

Thank fuck.

Grant keeps going, pounding into me as the orgasm fades. I recover enough to pull him back down against me, wrap my arms tight around his waist and pin him against me as I thrust up in time with him.

He speeds up, and his voice is throaty when he pulls me hard against his chest to growl against my ear, "I'm going to come. I'm going to fill your pussy with my cum, Sasha."

"Come in me, Grant," I gasp, pulling him closer, tight against me, his hard muscles slick with sweat, his body hard everywhere I'm soft. "Fuck yes. Fill me up," I moan.

His hands tighten almost painfully on my hips, and with a few last thrusts, he groans my name and comes hard, still pumping into me as he finishes. I thrust up against him and tighten my pussy muscles, contracting around him to milk every last drop of hot, wet, cum from his thick cock. He moans when I squeeze him, so I do it again, and he growls, pulling me so hard against him that I can hardly breathe for a second.

When he finishes thrusting, he lies along my body, our sweat mingling. I can feel his pulse in my chest, and it echoes my own, both racing hard as hell.

He draws back just far enough to look between us, and slowly, slowly draws his cock out of me. He's still huge, even now, and I gasp with a faint pang as he pulls out of me—I loved the feeling of having him inside me, feeling so full.

There's a hot rush as his cum trickles out, mingled with my own juices, and rushes down my thigh. I gasp softly, and Grant grins, glancing from that back to me.

"That's the only way to fuck," he says. "Raw and real."

My pussy aches—a bone deep ache that I fucking love. It's the feeling of having been thoroughly fucked, harder than I've ever been fucked before. I feel satisfied, in a way I've never known.

"Fuck yeah it is," I whisper, the loudest I can make my voice go now, my throat raw from the screams earlier.

Grant catches my eye and smiles. For a moment, I think I catch something else in it. Something more than just lust.

Then he lies back in bed beside me. I stretch out too, staring at the ceiling for a quiet moment until he reaches across to pull me against his side. I roll over and let him spoon me, his big, strong arms comforting, safe and secure.

I fall asleep with my head pillowed on his bicep, feeling the slow, steady rise and fall of his chest against my back, and all I can feel in that moment is completely and utterly content.

Chapter 7

Sasha Bluebell

I wake up alone. That doesn't seem strange at all—it's pretty normal for me, actually, par for the course. Until I stretch, and my whole body screams in aching protest, and I remember what the hell actually happened last night.

Fuck.

I roll over and check the bed beside me. It's empty. Cold. But right there on my side of the bed is a wet little puddle, the evidence of what we did last night. It's mostly dried now, but I can't help staring at it, wondering if I'm a complete idiot. I'm on birth control of course, but what was I thinking? I barely know Grant. I don't know if I should be fucking him—how did he put it?

A shiver runs down my spine at the memory. *Raw.*

But it feels better that way, I have to admit.

It felt *right* having him inside me, nothing between us. Feeling his hot cum fill me up.

I rub my temples and sit up. My ass and my pussy protest with an aching throb. Yep, he was true to his word. He definitely fucked me so hard that I'm going to have trouble walking today, let alone finishing yard work.

Not that I'm complaining. I'll take that ache any day. When I clench my pussy, the pressure makes me feel as though he's still inside me. It's the echo of the sensation of his wide girth filling me up, and I fucking love it, I can't lie.

I roll out of bed and sleepily reach for my suitcase. I should probably unpack it, I think, before I remember with a faint pang that I'll be leaving again in just four days now anyway, so what's the point?

Four days. Can we really get this farm back in shape in less than a week?

What do I do if we can't? Ask for more time off work? My boss would let me, but... Do I really want to spend more time here than I need to? More time in this crappy little town that I couldn't wait to escape as a kid, and that I can't wait to get out of all over again as an adult?

Hell no. I'm just going to have to step up my game. Work as hard as I'm playing.

But something about the thought of leaving makes my chest feel funny now. Before, all I wanted to do was run. Now... I don't know.

I shake my head. I'm just being ridiculous. One good fuck and I want to hang out in this Podunk place longer? What am I thinking?

I grab a change of clothes and pad out to the shower. The house is empty, silent, even though the roosters outside are only shrieking about dawn just now. Grant wakes up *early*, even for a country man.

In the bathroom, I squint at my reflection. My hair is an absolute mess, and I still smell like a mix of sweat and sex after last night. But there's an undeniable shine in my eyes, color in my cheeks. The look of a girl who's recently had the fuck of her life.

I exchange a grin with the girl in the mirror and turn the water on hot. As I soap up, I brush my fingertips over my mound, and suppress a gasp. Yeah, definitely sore. But that lovely, deep, aching kind of sore that reminds me all over again how fucking fantastic last night felt.

I can't stop picturing Grant above me in bed, his body arched over mine. The way he grabbed me and picked me up off the bed like I was weightless. The way he claimed me, fucked me hard and possessively, and came inside me, no shame about it. Just like the big rough and ready Country Man he is.

My heart starts beating faster, and I have to slide a hand between my legs just from thinking too hard about last night, a curl of pleasant memories tingling in my brain.

I stroke my clit, but even the lightest touch makes it flare red-hot. So I tease my fingertips across my mound, pressing just hard enough to turn my clit on without pushing too hard or getting sore.

All the while, I picture Grant fingering me. The way he rolled straight over and claimed my pussy without any hesitation. I picture him storming in here right now and taking me all over again in the shower, pinning me against the wall as he fingers me.

My clit throbs again, and I add a second finger, rubbing just hard enough to get my legs trembling, my knees shaking and my breath coming fast. When I come, I have to sag against the shower wall to hold myself up, and there's another rush as my juices, mingled with what was left of Grant's cum inside me, rush down my inner leg. I groan aloud, loving that hot sensation, loving the feeling that he was still inside me.

I finish washing, and once I've toweled off, I feel steady enough to walk at least semi-normally, though my legs still have a tendency to bow outward, a telltale giveaway of exactly what we were up to last night.

Not to mention I was already sore from the farm work.

Well, I'll just get more sore today, I resolve. So I might as well get used to it.

I dress in my now-favorite jean shorts and another throwaway T-shirt, one of the many ragged ones I brought with me on this trip, intending to throw them away at the end. I hadn't worn jeans and a T-shirt this often since… Well, I can't even remember now. But there's something relaxing about it. Something that feels really at home, no matter how much I don't want to admit it.

Like returning from a long vacation to find your familiar old comfy clothes right where you left them.

Except this isn't a return from vacation for me. This is just a break in my normal life. I remind myself of that as I stride out into the kitchen.

Once again, there's already a pot of coffee brewed and some rolls out by the microwave. I grab one and pour two cups of coffee this time, checking out the kitchen window.

It doesn't take me long to spot Grant. He's set up next to the shed today, ripping up the fence that borders the house to replace the posts. There's a stack of new posts beside him, and some wire to run between them. He's about halfway done.

I shake my head, in awe of how fast this man works. Then I scoop up both cups of coffee and pad out barefoot into the yard.

"Grant," I call.

He turns, glances over his shoulder.

I lift the second cup. "Re-up?" I ask.

He smiles and runs a hand through his hair, turning away from the fence and setting down the post holer he'd been using.

He jogs across the grass to my side, and I pass him the cup, sneaking a peek at his white tank top, which sticks to his sweat-slicked muscles as he leans back to take a long drink of the coffee.

I fucked him last night, I think, a thrill sparking through my body. My belly tightens with pleasure at the thought.

Then he finishes drinking and I quickly tear my gaze away, back to the fence, sipping from my mug as well. "Finished the roof already?" I ask when we've both taken a few more sips.

"Yesterday," he nods. "While you were resting."

"Thank you." I bite my lip and catch his eye. "I... Sorry again about that."

"Don't be," he says, his voice fierce and sincere. It's so vehement that I don't even try to argue with him this time. I just bow my head in agreement and take another sip of coffee.

"Need any help with these?" I ask, nodding at the fences.

He shakes his head. "I'm good on these." Before I can butt in and insist that I want to help— that this is as much my project as his, if not more so, since it's my mother's farm we're fixing up. His dad just bought into it was all—he seems to preempt my argument. "I had planned to start on the house itself soon, though," he says. "Repaint the rooms now that the electrical wiring's done, and get a head start on the gardens out front."

"That gate too," I say. "And the porch, the tire swing…"

"What's wrong with the tire swing?" he responds, almost defensive. I blink, startled.

"Nothing, just… It's ancient. The rope has got to be rotten through by now. It can't be safe."

He shakes his head. "Some things don't need changing, you know. You can leave some stuff be."

I raise an eyebrow. "What's so special about that one swing?"

"Nothing!" He groans and takes another long drink of his coffee. "Never mind. Forget it."

"Grant—"

"There's a party tonight," he says, startling me.

I blink up at him for a few seconds in silence, not exactly sure how I'm supposed to respond to that. "Okay?"

"Would you like to come with me?"

I let that hang for a moment. *He wants to spend time with me,* thinks one part of my brain. *He wants to be seen with me in public*, thinks another part. Even after yesterday. Even after everything. But still... I bite the inside of my cheek, thinking about what kind of party it could possibly be in a town like this. "You don't seem like the partying type," I say after a moment, mostly to stall.

"Normally I'm not," he replies simply.

I lift an eyebrow. "Is this a special occasion then?"

"I'm normally not the partying type," he clarifies. "But I *am* the attend-a-local-social-event-with-a-sexy-as-hell-woman-on-my-arm type."

"Ah." I grin a little more deeply. "Well, in that case... I'd love to go."

His smile deepens, just for a second. "Good." Then he turns his back to set down his coffee cup on the back table and dust off his hands.

"Well. I should get back to work."

"I should *start* work," I reply with a sigh. "I don't know how you get up and at it this early."

"Stamina," he calls over his shoulder with a wink.

My cheeks flare red, even as I smirk back at him and scoop up his cup to bring it inside. Out front, I stand and confront the mess of the front yard. Right. To work it is.

I lose track of the hours, elbow-deep in grease as I am. I oiled and cleaned and adjusted the front gate until it shone, until there wasn't a single speck of rust on the whole thing and it swings open and shut without so much as a squeak or a creak.

Then I weeded the front garden, a little patch of flowers and herbs that Mama used to keep around for cooking. There are still a few surviving ones, so I pick some fresh basil and oregano for dinner tonight. I figure if Grant wants to eat before this party, whatever it is, we can whip up a simple chicken dinner with the oregano, and I'll make a side salad with the basil and some veggies.

God, listen to me. I'm starting to sound like a country bumpkin. Like a housewife.

Like my mother, part of my brain calls out, and for a second, I pause in my work to wonder if that would really be so bad. Living life her way. Mama was always happy. She didn't love that I hated this town so much, of course. And while she visited me plenty in NYC, I could tell she didn't love the city itself. But every time I'd talk to her, she'd be bursting with excitement over something. A new flower that took in the garden, a new dish she figured out how to cook, a new friend she made in town, whatever hapless new neighbor had just moved nearby enough for Mama to latch on and start introducing them to everyone in sight. She was a social butterfly, my Mama, country girl or no.

A life like that might not be so bad, I find

myself thinking.

But. I remind myself why that was our life. We didn't have any choice. Not after my father up and abandoned us both. Ran away, left Mama brokenhearted, a heartbreak she never really recovered from enough to date again. And left me holding the pieces together for years, until she finally healed enough to feel okay. She was happy in her later years, content without a partner, but still…

I shake my head.

Not to mention how *I* felt… But no.

I don't go there. Not anymore. Not ever.

I finish weeding just as a clatter inside lets me know Grant is stomping around the house. He sticks his head out the front door long enough to holler, "Lunch is on the table," then he's gone again.

I bag up the weeds and dust my knees off, then head inside the house to find fresh sandwiches on the counter and a salad full of veggies he clearly harvested from the farm out back.

"You really need to let me cook sometime," I call in the general direction of the shower, where I can hear him puttering.

"Dinner tonight then," he replies. "If you insist."

"I do," I answer, grinning.

"Fair enough." He pops his head out of the bathroom, and I have to suck in a breath at the sight of his shirtless chest. *Damn*. The perfection of those muscles manages to shock me every damn time. "Make it 7 though, cause the party starts at 8."

"What kind of party are we talking exactly?" I ask, digging into my sandwich. It's nothing complex, but it's delicious nonetheless. Simple, fresh ingredients. Just the way I like it.

"Nothing big. Just a little get-together over at the Johnsons' farm."

I mull that over while I chew a big bite of lettuce. By then, Grant is back at the table with me, scooping up his own sandwich and taking a huge bite while he pours a glass of water. He plunks that down in front of me with a significant, pointed look, and my cheeks flush at the memory of yesterday. Sufficiently cowed, I accept the water and take a long gulp.

"You sure you want to be seen with me in public around here?" I ask with a smirk. "I'm not exactly on the county's most popular list."

"I went out with you yesterday, didn't I?" he points out, and I have to give him that one.

"Social event will be different though," I say. "Yesterday you could write off as a work necessity. This is voluntary."

"Yeah," he agrees. "I know." He locks eyes with me for a long moment, and my heart leaps against my throat. But before I can ask anything else, he finishes the last of his sandwich in one huge bite. "Seven work for dinner?" he asks as he shoves his way out the back door once more.

"See you then," I confirm as the door swings shut between us. Then I dust off my own hands and get back to work.

Chapter 8

Sasha Bluebell

Dinner turns out great. I make chicken oregano and Caprese salad, which Grant has never had before. He didn't exactly gush about the homemade pesto sauce I mixed in for added flavor, but he definitely helped himself to four servings, then admitted between bites that it was "addictive."

There was something weirdly calm, almost familiar, about sitting across the dinner table from Grant and chatting about the day. He told me all the progress he'd made, and any problems he'd run up against, and I did the same. We charted out plans for the rest of the week, what we'd aim to fix up and what we were okay with letting go. It felt weirdly... *fun*, to plan like that. To tackle a problem like this, a simple, concrete problem that we could fix with our hands.

Nothing at all like my usual work

explosions, which have twelve different possible solutions, half of which depend on other people in the office who are unreliable.

That, and it helps that the whole time we're talking, his hand keeps brushing past mine, his knee touching mine under the table, both of us cracking flirtatious jokes that make me blush and him smirk wider, a look that says he has plans for me later tonight…

Then he takes over the dishes—he insists—and I slip out to my room to change for the party. After digging through my suitcase, I settle on the little black dress that I packed—just in case, I'd figured when I was tossing half my NYC closet into this suitcase. *Thanks a million, past Sasha*, I think as I pull it on and turn before the bedroom mirror, grateful for the thinking ahead.

This dress is one of my favorites at home. It's chic, stylish, and couture. It hugs my every curve, showing off my slim waist and my hips to perfection. There's beading along the chest, hugging the neckline, which plunges just far enough to hint at cleavage without revealing too much. In the back, the skirt hugs my thighs tight, shows off my pert ass.

I twirl a little in front of the mirror and grin. *Perfect.*

Pair that with a pair of heels—not the mud-stained pair I tripped in on day one, but the backup pair of Manolos, neon red heels flashing under the sleek black-and-silver top halves. Then I just have to do my makeup—I keep it simple, mascara, cat eyes, and a hint of gold lipstick that lets the rest of my outfit speak for itself—and shift my possessions into the little silver clutch purse I brought, the one shaped like an old Cuban cigar case.

I twirl before the mirror, loving the effect I have. I look like a million bucks. I look like my old self, my New York self. I look ready to slay whatever this party holds.

I stride out of my room into the hallway. Grant, for his part, is already waiting by the door, truck keys in hand. Oh no.

"I'll drive," I say before he even looks up from his phone, which he's checking for his usual once-a-day stop to make sure he hasn't missed anything.

When he does look up at last, his eyes do a slow, steady sweep of my body that sends shivers down my spine. When those eyes finally lock back onto mine, he's grinning, a sly, knowing look. "Are you trying to skip this party tonight?" he asks.

"What?" I frown. "No, why?"

His grin widens. "Because wearing that makes me want to throw you over my shoulder and drag you right back into the bedroom," he says.

My legs clench, as the shivers race all the way down into my pussy. *So let's,* I almost say, but Grant doesn't give me time. He's already opening the front door and holding it for me to pass, half-bowing at the waist, ever the gentleman.

"After you," he says.

Only then do I really take in his outfit, and

remember where the hell I am.

He looks good, don't get me wrong. He looks hot as hell, actually, in clean black jeans and a loose V-neck gray T-shirt. But he doesn't look like this is a *party* party. At least not the kind that I'm used to.

But of course it isn't. I'm not in New York. I'm in my hometown, home to no more than 2,000 residents max. I wince. "Crap," I say, hesitating.

"Forget something?" His eyebrows rise.

"No, I just…" I shake my head and stare down at myself. "Should I change?"

"Are you kidding?" Grant snorts. "You look beautiful, Sasha. You always do."

"I'm going to stand out though. In this."

He lifts an eyebrow. "You were always going to stick out, Sasha. No matter what you wear. You stick out anywhere you go—I'd wager you stick out just as much back in the big city as you do here. A girl like you couldn't help it." His dark eyes latch onto mine, keep hold. "And I love that about

157

you." With that, he offers his arm, bent at the elbow. "Now, are we going to go be the talk of the town, or am I going to have to drag you back into the bedroom to peel that excuse for a dress off?" He says it with a grin though, eyes appreciative as they dip across my body again, and my belly tightens with anticipation.

I hook my arm through his. "If we go to this party, does that mean you won't peel this dress off me later? Because I was rather looking forward to that. Not sure I can get out of it all on my own…"

He laughs softly as he leads me outside and lets the door swing shut behind us. "Don't worry, Sasha. One way or another, I mean to have you tonight." He leans in close to kiss the edge of my earlobe, then nips at the skin lightly, just hard enough to make me gasp, before he whispers, breath hot on my neck, "Wherever that may be."

I shiver and lean into him, already feeling the throb of my hungry clit between my thighs. "I'll hold you to that promise," I warn him.

"I would expect nothing less." He winks, and opens the passenger side door of the truck. But I shake my head this time and pull out my clutch.

"My car this time." I grin at his wide-eyed expression. "If we're going to be the talk of the town," I say, "we're going to do it in style."

It takes my poor rental Porsche a while to ease back down the dirt driveway. But as soon as we hit pavement and Grant's able to direct me toward the Johnsons' farmstead, I really gun it. A smile creeps onto my face as I take the back-road country highway by storm, letting this car do what it was built to do—dominate the road.

Grant laughs over the country music blasting on the radio—because I changed the channel to his the moment I turned it on. What can I say? Something about the old nostalgic beats got me going.

"Didn't take you for a speed demon," he calls.

"Yeah, well, you don't know everything

about me, Grant Werther," I toss back with a smirk.

"Not yet," he rejoins, and just that simple promise makes me shiver all over again.

We race along the back roads, and it takes no time at all going the speed I'm doing to reach the Johnsons'. As soon as we get close, though, I can already tell where we're heading. It's the only place for miles around with its lights on, and a few big tents out back, all illuminated by candles and bonfires and a few stoves out on the back patio. There must be fifty cars all up and down their driveway. Small party by NYC standards, but a regular who's-who of the whole town for these parts.

I whip into a spot at the head of the drive, and Grant hops out too fast for me to slow him down. Fast enough to swing around and open my door and offer me a hand. *That man is never going to stop doing that, is he?* I wonder as I accept his help and climb out beside him, purse clutched under my arm.

I loop my other arm through Grant's and follow him up the driveway toward the distant music. It sounds a lot like what was just on the radio actually—only louder, and faster, and, if I'm not mistaken, live.

"Is that a band?" I ask as we reach the front yard. But Grant skips right past the front door and heads for the back. I'd forgotten what is was like in a small town. Just walking right inside like you own places.

"Few of the local guys get together once a month to play. In the summers, the couples and families like to come out and do a turn together while they listen. But this'll be the last hoedown of the season, so near about everyone's turned out for it."

We round the corner then, and my eyes widen. He wasn't kidding.

At least 150 people are around—kids racing underfoot, chasing one another across the grass, couples up on the dance floor in front of the 4-

person string band, doing a complicated square dance that I vaguely recognize from old school dances, though Lord help me if I remember the steps. Still more people are dotted across the yard, some playing lawn darts, another group lined up by the garage playing regular darts against its closed door. Between those two groups, set up under the tents on the tail end of the driveway, are a couple of pool tables.

Both occupied at the moment, though my eyes linger on them for longer than strictly necessary. I always loved pool—played it as a way to escape when I was younger, back when Dad was still around, when he'd get into his rages. Then I kept playing through college, mostly because guys found it sexy. After college, I kept playing to dupe guys out of drinks in bars. Guess you could say I'm a regular shark about it.

I grin a little to myself. I'll have to challenge Grant to that later.

Grant, for his part, has drawn more than a

few stares and shouts of welcome as we walked in. He's waving back now, and gesturing from me to the crowd.

"Y'all will remember Sasha," he's saying, voice louder than I'd like, even with the music to cover some of it. "Maryanne's girl. Sasha, this is…" He trails off with a shrug. "Well, everyone."

A couple nearby laugh.

Across the yard, I recognize Hank and Etna from the hardware store, deep in conversation with another couple their age. Both of them are eating too, and drinking cans of the local cheap beer I grew up on before I went away to college and learned what real alcohol tasted like.

For some reason, though, watching them, my taste buds are suddenly craving that flavor. That familiar sour tang.

"Want a beer?" Grant asks, following my gaze. Most of the people he just introduced us to have gone back to their meals or conversations, though a few are still stealing surreptitious glances at me from underneath their eyelashes every now and again.

"Sure," I reply, forcing a wide smile. I'm regretting my dress choice already—hell, maybe the choice to come here at all was a bad one. I should have just let Grant drag me into the bedroom and fuck me all night again. That would be far preferable to being stared at like I'm on display right now.

But as we drift across the room, beers in hand, and settle at a table by the dance floor, some of the stares drift away and drop off. One girl even leans over from a neighboring table to tap my shoulder and smile at me broadly. "Love your dress," she whispers.

"Thanks." I offer a hand. "Sasha, by the way."

"Meredith. You new here too?" she asks.

Ah. Well that would explain the lack of an attitude. My cheeks flush, even as I shrug my shoulders. "Uh… Kind of? It's a long story."

Luckily Meredith doesn't press for details. "I moved back here with Joe after we finished school." She nudges the guy across the table from her, who starts out of a conversation he's in with a neighbor for long enough to grin and wave.

"Where are you from originally?" I ask, turning to loop Grant in, only to find he's been caught in a different conversation with a guy I vaguely recognize. Tommy? No. Trent? Something with a T...

"Philly," she replies. "So, you know, bit different than this." She gestures at the party with her beer and laughs softly.

My eyes widen. "Wasn't that hard, then? Going from a big city to... well. This?"

Meredith laughs. "Hell no. Best decision I ever made. I was a mess up in the northeast. I know that pace of life, that speed, it's right for some people, but for me, it just made me anxious 24/7. I felt like I always had to be on, on, on, couldn't ever take time to breathe or relax. And life was just flying by. Here… Well. Life here moves at its own pace. Slower. More sedate. I like that." She smiles and takes a long swig of her beer.

I sip mine too. It tastes familiar. Not hoppy or unique like a lot of the local brews I drink back in the city, all the fancy ones breweries in Brooklyn are always coming up with. It just tastes simple. Easy to drink.

It tastes like home, I realize with a start.

"I can understand that," I hear myself saying. But then Grant taps me on the shoulder, and Meredith winks and turns back to Joe, and I spin to attend to my guy.

My guy? Is he that?

I shake that thought off.

"Sasha, you'll remember Troy," Grant says.

Troy. "Of course," I reply, grinning as we shake hands. "You were in my English class senior year right? The one who made all those paper plane notes to throw at… Oh gosh, what was her name?"

"Sarah." Troy's smile widens, turns genuine

when he realizes that I do remember him after all.

"Sarah, that's right. How'd that turn out?"

He laughs. "Well, I married her, so guess for yourself." He leans down to elbow me slightly. "But personally, I'd say it went pretty damn all right."

Grant's watching me interact with Troy, something like approval in his eye. I flash a small smile back at Grant, relaxing a little.

Okay, maybe not everyone in town is a jerk. Or at least, once I get to know them—or re-know them—they stop assuming they know everything about me. I could get used to that. Not being a total pariah.

"So how about you Sasha?" Troy asks. "I hear you've been living up in New York City now. Big shot in advertising, right?"

I shake my head. "Paralegal. But I'm really just a glorified desk jockey, that's all."

"Don't sell yourself short," Grant cuts in, eyes locked on mine. "Your career is really important to you, isn't it?"

167

I chew on the inside of my lip. Of course it was. Is. I just hadn't realized until I took this break away from the desk—until I was staying somewhere without Wi-Fi —how much of my life it consumes. Hell, I haven't checked my email once since I got here.

Just thinking about that now sends a spark of panic through me. God, the pile that's going to be awaiting me when I get back on Monday…

But I don't want to think about that now. I don't *have* to think about that now, because for once in my damn life, I'm unplugged. Really and truly unplugged.

"Well, who wants to talk about work when they're on vacation?" I push to my feet and reach for Grant's hand. "Dance?"

Troy tips his hat to us and steps aside as Grant accepts my hand, then tugs me to his side and leads me to the dance floor.

"You call this a vacation?" he asks as we line up for the next square dance, in a pattern I don't know. "Working your ass off to fix up a farmhouse, that's your break, really?"

I shrug. "It's hard to get time off. Schedules are packed around this time of year—end of summer, you know, everyone wants to live up the last days of warmth."

"And you're spending them back home in the town you hated, doing hard labor with a business partner you never wanted," he supplies.

The band strikes up a tune. Grant plants a firm hand on my hip and guides me into position across from him.

"I don't remember—" I start to say, then cut off with a gasp when he pulls me straight into a fast, side-stepping swing.

"Just relax and follow me," he says, rocking through the steps with an easy gait, pulling me along with him.

I promptly step on his foot, then stumble trying to catch my footing again. He tightens his grip on my waist, pulls me closer, until I can feel the heat radiating from him, our bodies almost touching.

"I said relax," he points out, and I flush, biting my lip.

"That's hard when I don't know what I'm doing," I mumble.

"You have to give up control, Sasha. You have to trust me. Because *I* know what I'm doing." He locks eyes with me, and for a second, I have the sensation that we're talking about more than just this dance.

I hold his gaze when he starts to move again. I try my best to listen to his advice—to forget about my footing, the pace, the song. To just watch him, feel his one big hand wrapped around mine, his other cupping my waist, drawing me across the floor.

When I keep my eyes on him, I find it's easier to let go. Easier to let him take control, to read his body to learn what he wants mine to do.

Pretty soon, we're flying across the floor

easily. He swings me out away from him, then spins me back in to his side, and someone behind us whoops. There's other dancers on the floor now, but we're weaving between them, lost in a world of our own. I have eyes only for Grant. For a big man, he sure does move lightly on his feet. He dances like he was born doing it, and I'm just along for the ride.

Without warning, at a peak moment in the song, he grabs me and dips me backwards across his forearm. I gasp as I fall back against his arm, but he's got me, holding me up as easily as though I weighed nothing at all.

I catch his eye again, and catch a hint of that hungry expression, the one that shows me just how much he can't get enough of me. How much he wants to claim me.

It sends an ache through my body, makes me just as hungry for him. Having his strong arms around me, feeling the way he can fling me across this dance floor, it's turning me on way too much to be appropriate in public.

And, judging by the hard press I feel against my thigh when he swings me back upright and pulls me flush against him for the final chords of the song, he's feeling the same way.

The music fades, and for the span of a second, it's just the two of us. His heartbeat pounding against mine as we stand there, chest-to-chest, arms around one another—when did that happen? My head swims, fuzzy with desire. There are people talking, laughing, slapping one another on the shoulders. From the corner of my eye I notice people watching us, whispers starting. I don't care. I have eyes only for Grant.

He smirks and turns away to lead me off the floor, though he keeps his hand wrapped around mine long after we leave the dance floor behind.

"Think we've started enough rumors yet?" I ask in a soft voice as we cross the tent. He stops by the coolers propped at the far end to grab another beer and tosses me a mischievous grin along with a second beer.

"Far from it."

I glance past him at the rest of the tent. It feels like everyone in here is staring at me now—but maybe that's just my imagination.

"They're not as bad as you think, you know," Grant murmurs beside my ear, so close that a shiver runs down my back. I can feel his hot breath on my cheek, and that combined with the memory of his arms around me, the hard press of his cock through his jeans when we ended that dance, it makes me feel horny as a teenager at her first school dance. I want to grab him and drag him into the trees around this field, rip those jeans off.

My cheeks flare bright red. "They're staring," I point out, my voice low.

"Only because you're worth looking at." He smirks, then his eyes dart past me for a second. "Game?"

For a moment, I don't understand what he means. Then I follow his gaze to the nearest pool table, now empty of players. I smirk, too. "You're on."

Those staring spectators don't dissipate as we cross to pick up our cues. If anything, the crowd grows. By the time Grant breaks and lands two solid pockets in a row, there's an actual audience standing around our table.

"Have you warned your new girl you're a shark at this game, Werther?" one of the guys comments, strolling over to join the slowly growing spectators around our table.

Grant snorts, but misses his next shot, and I grin as the cue ball lines up perfectly with a stripe in the corner pocket. I sink that, then two more, one after another, my smirk widening with every shot. By the third, the crowd is whooping.

"Guess the shark has met his match," the guy amends, and Grant locks eyes with me, a challenge in his dark gaze.

I toss my head, beaming now. "Or there's a new shark in town." With that, I sink my fourth ball in a row, and exchange celebratory high-fives with a few guys who offer their palms. Troy has joined the crowd now, and Meredith, along with her husband, Joe.

"Kick his ass, Sasha," Meredith calls, and I wink at her as I line up my next shot.

But I must be getting too confident, too fast, because the next shot misses. And it lines Grant's next move up perfectly. Damn. I bite my lip and step away as I wait for him to fire.

He pockets another ball. I swallow hard. He lands another one after that, and I realize it's time to whip out the big guns.

I step closer to the table and lean down to watch his next shot, right in his line of vision.

He glances up to line up the balls, and then his eyes dart to me. To my cleavage, showing just below the neckline of my dress. All he'll be able to glimpse from his angle is a hint of red lace, the edge of my bra, and a little bit of the cleavage it's pushing up to my advantage.

But apparently it's enough.

Grant fires and misses completely, scratching the ball.

The whoops around us intensify, and a few guys slap Grant on the back.

"Losing your touch, man," Troy teases him as I toss the cue ball in my palm, debating where to line up.

"And to a city girl, no less," I add, batting my lashes with faux innocence.

The look in his eyes is half annoyance, half furious desire. "What can I say?" he replies, a cool smile on his mouth. "I don't have the same bag of tricks up my sleeve." He does, however, lean against the table as I set up my next shot, making sure to stretch his arms wide enough that it pulls his T-shirt taut, shows off the outline of his muscles beneath, every sexy inch of them.

I tear my gaze away, forcing my head into the game. I pocket my next two balls. Down to just one and the 8-ball left.

"What do you say we up the stakes?" Grant

asks, his voice low.

A couple of whistles steal through the crowd anyway.

I lift an eyebrow. "What did you have in mind?"

"I win, you have to do everything I say for the next hour."

The crowd titters with laughter. He, however, has his dark eyes fixed straight on me, dead serious. And I know exactly what he's thinking.

A trickle of desire runs down my spine. I imagine myself doing his bidding. Whatever he commands...

I raise my chin and lock eyes with him. "And if I win?"

"Then same. You make the rules."

"Do it," Troy shouts.

"Make that boy your bitch," Meredith adds, and I laugh, watching her and Joe elbow one another after that comment.

I tap my chin with the pool cue, as though debating. But really, all I can think about is what it would be like to be *his* for an hour. Forced to obey his every command, his every whim… It's almost enough to make me want to lose on purpose.

Almost.

But then I think about being the one in charge of this big, sexy country boy, and I change my mind. Hell no. I want to win this thing. If for nothing more than to see what I can make this big man do to me…

"You're on," I tell him, and his grin widens.

I'm not sure why until I study the table again. Crap. My next shot is tricky as hell. I'll have to bank the cue ball twice just to hit my ball, let alone sink it. I take a deep breath and line up. I have to block out the chants that the crowd has started—*Bust him, Bluebell,* in particular, has become a fast favorite apparently.

I shoot, but the second my stick hits the ball, I realize I've messed up. It banks off the wall too sharply, and misses my shot entirely.

Grant's smile widens.

I swallow hard. He lines up his next play. I watch him sink his fifth and sixth balls without too much worry. But as he lines up an easy shot for his seventh, my nerves start to jangle.

Shameless by this point, I hike up the edge of my dress and take a seat across from him on the table. A few of the guys wolf whistle. Grant fixes his gaze on me and smirks.

"Not going to save you this time," he says.

I narrow my eyes. "Worth a shot," I shrug, letting a finger trail up my outer thigh. "You know. Just in case you're easily distracted…"

He fires the next shot, and the ball hits the pocket straightaway. Shit.

He just has the eight ball left.

The crowd, at least, seems to be on my side. I laugh as chants of *Miss, Miss, Miss* replace the old Bluebell cry. Maybe Grant's friends just want to see him lose a game for once, but for me, it almost makes me feel like I belong here for a moment.

Almost.

Unfortunately, Grant doesn't take the crowd's advice. He calls the eight ball pocket, and I watch with my heart in my throat as it glides right in on his first try.

I swallow hard around the lump.

"Good game," Grant says, hand extended.

I lock eyes with him as I grasp his hand. "You too." His grip tightens, and I enjoy the warm sensation of his fingers wrapped around mine.

Then he lets go, as the crowd begins to dissipate a little, spectators drifting off to watch another pool match starting up at the other table. Troy slaps my back as he passes, and shoots me a commiserating smile. "Almost had him," he says. "Next time."

"Well," I say to Grant, lifting my chin to meet his gaze. "Congratulations, big winner. What happens now?"

"Now?" His smile deepens. "I believe by the

terms of our agreement, you owe me an hour."

"Mmhmm. And just what did you have in mind for this hour of being the boss, exactly?"

His gaze drops down my body, tracing the outlines of my curves. Then he leans down to whisper against my ear, so no one else can hear, his breath so hot it makes my belly tighten with desire. "Meet me behind the tents in five minutes and find out." With that, he strides away and leaves me holding my cold beer, heart racing, panties already in danger of getting far too wet for a public setting.

"Tough luck," Meredith says as she reaches my side through the crowd, slapping me on the shoulder.

I shrug. "You win some, you lose some."

"Still, you play great. Where'd you learn to shoot pool like that?"

I grimace, and repress the memory as fast as I can. Me escaping Dad's shouts in the farmhouse, hiding out in the toolshed with the toy pool table Dad made me when he was in one of his better moods, way back when.

"Around," I reply.

"Who knew New York could handle bar games that well," Joe, Meredith's husband, comments with a laugh. He doesn't seem judgmental though, just stating a fact.

I put a hand on my hip. "We do have bars up in the big city, you know," I point out. "And parties too. Even backyard hoedowns in some places." I gesture around us.

"Not like ours," he counters, and I have to concede that point. I haven't been to anything quite like this party up in the city.

"There are some things I miss about life here," I admit, turning to take in the tent. The kids are back, taking over the dance floor now. My heart nearly stops as I watch a little curly blonde girl grab a brunette boy's hand and drag him onto the floor, trying to teach him the steps to a dance her mother and father are doing right next to her. *I remember times like that.* Back when we were all here. Back when we were still a family. Not just Mama and me, left on our own. Left to heal the rift without any help.

"You'd be surprised how nice it can be," Meredith is saying, leaning against Joe as he loops one arm around her shoulders. "The quiet might seem suffocating when you first come from the big city, all that hustle and bustle. But give it enough time to get into your bones and…" She sighs, smiling. "You can really get used to a life like this. A slower life. A sweeter one."

"Careful, honey." Joe squeezes Meredith's shoulders. "You'll give the girl a cavity with all that sweet-talking."

She elbows him, and I grin at their interplay. Which reminds me. I glance past them, but can't find a clock anywhere in this tent. Still, my five minutes are probably almost up. "I'll be back," I tell them, and I don't miss the telltale smirk that Meredith sports when I step away, toward the tent flap.

I have a feeling the two of them know what Grant was doing when he proposed that bet over the pool game.

Hell, most people here must guess. That only makes my cheeks flare hotter when I slip out into the cool night air and circle around toward the back of the tent. There's a few people dotted across the grass back here, some smoking, others just standing around chatting, beers in hand. I weave between them, farther and farther away from the tent, until I recognize a familiar shape leaning against the side of the small farmhouse out beyond the little tent village set up for this party. That must be the Johnsons' actual house. To my surprise, I recognize it. Well, not the house itself, but the porch out front with a big rocker swing on it, and hard-to-forget neon orange cushions. I've sat out here with Mama before, visiting.

"If you're aiming for inconspicuous, this might not be the best place," I call as I approach Grant. There are still plenty of people around us, chatting, hanging out. I can practically feel the gazes following us.

But when I reach his side, Grant just tilts his head toward me, a sly look in his eye. "Who said we're stopping here?" He reaches out and slaps my ass before he walks away, past the house, toward the backyard. "Try to keep up. I only have an hour with you. I plan to make the best of that time."

I jog after him with a huff. "Some of us didn't plan on hiking through yards in our outfits for the night," I protest under my voice as my heels threaten to sink into the muddy ground.

He heaves a sigh. Then, without another word, he scoops me up into his arms, even as I squeal in protest.

"I'm in charge now, Sasha," he reminds me, his voice a low rumble against my chest, cradled as I am against his. "And you won't deny me what I want, will you?" His voice thrums with promise, all the things he wants to do to me.

I have to admit that I'm getting wetter just

thinking about it. "No," I murmur, my protest subsiding as he continues pacing across the grass, far beyond the house. I want to ask where we're going. The party isn't in sight anymore, though neither is much else out here, alone in the moonlit fields.

But then he turns away from the grass, toward the edge of the lawn, where there's a copse of trees, and my eyes widen.

There's something in the trees. A squat little construction that's hard to make out from here. Until we cross into the shadow of the canopy ourselves, and my eyes adjust to the dim. Then I recognize the outline, and my jaw drops.

There's a tree house here. Not a little play tree house either, like the kind we'd goof off in as kids. This one is shaped like an actual house, only held about 15 feet off the ground, with a staircase leading up to it that winds around the trunk of the tree.

"What...?" I ask, trailing off as Grant starts

up the steps without even breaking his stride.

"Airbnb," he explains, as though that tells me anything. I blink at him. He laughs. "Johnsons make extra renting this place out. A lot of people come to this area looking for escapes from cities, you know. A rustic country experience." We reach the door, and he shoulders it open easily. "A taste of country life."

It dawns on me, and my eyes widen. "You planned this," I accuse him, chin jutting out.

He swings me down and lands me on my feet lightly, amusement dancing in his gaze. "Not exactly. Not everything." He tilts his head and raises a brow. "I didn't know you'd accept that bet."

"You didn't know you'd win the game either," I point out, crossing my arms.

He shrugs. "I was fairly confident."

I snort.

He steps closer, eying me. "Even if you could've won, you wouldn't have." His eyes trace over me, so hot I can practically feel his gaze like a touch, even though he's still a foot away. "Because you want to be mine, Sasha. You want to know what I'll make you do."

My pussy tightens at those words. I can't exactly deny it. It's exactly what I was thinking when he made that bet. Still, I have some pride. I cross my arms and raise my chin. "What makes you so sure?"

He steps closer, and reaches out a finger to trace it up my arm. He trails it all the way up to my shoulder, then across my shoulder to cup my neck in his palm lightly. It takes every ounce of willpower I possess not to lean into that touch right now. "I can see it in your eyes. How much you want to be mine. My slave for the night."

I swallow hard against a tight lump in my throat. I'm soaking wet now, damn him, and he fucking knows it, to judge by his confident smirk.

"Isn't that right, city girl?"

I bite my lip. Hesitate. Then I finally inhale sharply and catch my breath. "I was curious, country boy."

"That's master to you. For the next hour." He grins, a spark in his eyes.

"I was curious… *Master*." I lean into the word, emphasize it with sarcasm. But there is something sexy about calling him that. Submitting to him completely.

"Kneel down," he says, and I glance down at the hardwood floors of the tree house. It's surprisingly cozy in here, a little bed in one corner, a cushy couch nearby. But the hard wood floor doesn't exactly look appealing. Grant follows my gaze and leans past me to grab a pillow from the couch, which he tosses at my feet.

I follow his order and drop to my knees on the pillow.

"Undo my jeans," he says.

I reach up for the button, toying with it for a moment, gazing up at him and memorizing this view. He towers over me from this angle, and something animal and instinctive in me loves that.

I undo the button and tease the moment out, taking my time pulling down his zipper. I can already feel the hard line of his cock through the thick denim. I draw the zipper down slowly, and his cock is so thick it pushes his boxers forward even before I pull his jeans down his hips.

"Take off my jeans."

I yank them down, until they puddle on the ground between his feet.

"Boxers too," he says, and I glance up to make eye contact before I slide those down, an inch at a time, slowly, taking my time. When his cock springs free at last, though, I have to catch my breath all over again at seeing him this close up.

His cock truly is fucking glorious. I reach up to touch him, to trace the veins that bulge along his sides, standing out against his rock hard shaft. But he clicks his tongue and stops me in my tracks.

"I didn't say to touch me yet," he scolds, and I sit back on my heels with a little pout, stealing a glance up at him. "Apologize."

190

"I'm sorry," I say, holding his gaze.

He raises an eyebrow. "I'm sorry, what?"

"I'm sorry, Master." That word sends another shiver into my belly, another rush in my veins.

"I want you to taste me, Sasha," he says, his voice low with suppressed desire.

I lean forward, my lips hovering an inch from his tip.

"Lick my cock."

I lick the tip of his cock with the flat blade of my tongue, and my whole body goes stiff with want. *Fuck*. He tastes *good*. Salty and earthy and all him, like his scent but magnified. I want more. I trail my tongue down the side of his shaft, first one, then the other, keeping my eyes fixed on him all the while, enjoying the view up along his washboard abs, visible through his tight T-shirt. Even better is the way he watches me explore him, his eyes hooded with desire as he focuses on what I'm doing.

"Play with my balls while you lick me," he says, and I'm all too eager to raise both hands and cup his balls between them, rolling his balls through my fingers as I continue to lick up and down his length, making him slick with my saliva.

"Slowly take me into your mouth," he says, and I know I'm not imagining the tightness in his voice, the way his control teeters on the edge. I want to make him lose control.

I part my lips and take his cock into my mouth. *Fuck.* He's huge. My jaw stretches to take him, but I just part my lips wider and swallow him deeper, pushing him inch by inch into my mouth. I want his cock inside me, as much as I can take. I want to get him off.

I lift my hands to encircle the base of his cock, and it takes both hands to wrap around him. I finally have him as deep in my mouth as I think he'll go, and I start to rock backward, but he reaches down and wraps his hands through my hair, tangling his fingers in my curls and pinning me in place.

"Have you ever tried deep-throat, Sasha?" he asks.

It's hard to reply with his cock in my mouth, but I manage an *uh-uh*, my voice muffled. He inhales sharply as the vibrations around his cock send shocks along his nerve system, and I make a mental note of that for later.

"Do you want to?"

Mmhmm, I agree, making sure to let the sound last, my mouth buzzing around his shaft. His cock jumps in my mouth, and I press my tongue along the underside of his shaft to keep up the pressure.

"Relax your jaw."

I do as I'm told, at least as much as I can. He presses forward, and I reach around to grab his ass with one hand, holding on as his cock slides toward the back of my tongue. My body tenses, and I feel my gag reflex start to kick in, but Grant is slow, patient. He draws back a little.

"Really relax, Sasha. Give me control."

I try to do that. This time, when he presses forward again, I take him deeper, deeper than I've ever been able to take any guy before. I let my jaw go limp, surrender control to Grant, to the taste of his big cock in my mouth, the feel of him filling me up. He hits the back of my throat, and I reach up to grab his ass with both hands, taking a deep breath before he presses down, into my throat. My lips almost touch his base, and he's as far down my throat as he can go, his head falling back, his teeth gritted.

"Fuck, Sasha," he hisses, and my stomach tightens at that sound, the sound of him lost in pleasure—*because of me.*

He draws back again, and I breathe in deep as soon as I can, his cock wet from my throat and tongue. I circle my tongue against his underside as he pulls out of my mouth, then slowly back in.

I can't get enough of this. Looking up at him and catching him watching me hungry, gaze hooded, his cock at attention in my mouth, his whole body taut with tension as he starts to rock back and forth, his hands tightening in my hair.

I can tell he's getting close as his muscles tense, and I lean into his motions, tightening my mouth around him, eager to make him lose control the way he makes me. A low groan escapes his mouth, and I moan in response, loving how he tenses, sucking in a sharp breath through his teeth.

But just when he's about to finish, he presses his palm against my forehead, halting me in place. "Not yet, Sasha." There's a strain in his voice —it's taking him effort not to let me finish. I stop moving, but I keep pressing my tongue along the underside of his cock, tracing the veins with the tip of my tongue. He inhales again, sharper.

"I want to enjoy you for longer," he murmurs, slowly drawing out of my mouth. When his cock passes my lips, I let out a soft sigh of protest, and he chuckles. "Eager to finish already?"

I shake my head, meeting his gaze. "I want to taste you."

He raises an eyebrow, pointed.

I swallow, catching his meaning. "I mean, I want to taste you... Master."

He grins. "Maybe I'll reward you after this with a taste of my cum. Would you like that, City Girl?"

"Yes, Master," I reply, not even hesitating this time, getting into character. There's something thrilling about this, about submitting.

His smile widens and he steps back. "Stand up."

I push myself to my feet, eyes still on his body, his cock at attention between us, demanding all of *my* attention.

"Take off your dress." I reach for the hem, but he stops me with a lifted palm. "Slowly."

So I lock eyes with him and take my time, sliding my dress up inch by inch, revealing more skin tantalizingly slowly. I step closer to him, making sure to lean into my step, sway my hips, and his gaze drops to them obediently, his eyes lingering on my curves with clear appreciation.

I drop my dress beside us, standing just an inch from his chest.

He raises his brows. "Now your bra."

I reach behind me with one hand to unclasp it, and let it inch down my arms until my breasts fall free. I love the way his eyes darken with hunger, focused on my chest.

He steps closer and lifts his hands to cup my hips gently, his skin white-hot against mine, his palms rough and calloused as they tug me against him. His cock digs into my stomach as he pulls me against his body, and slides his hands down, down, to the edges of my panties, where he hooks both thumbs under the sides.

"These I want to remove myself," he murmurs, face bent to inches from mine.

I tilt my head back to meet his eye, and he leans down to kiss me, hard. My lips part with surprise, and his tongue slides between them, tangling with mine, hungry, searching. I lift my arms, wrap them around his neck and sink into the kiss, letting him taste me, claim me, as he pushes my panties down my thighs. When they reach my knees, they drop to the floor, and I step out of them, still kissing him, as he pulls me backwards, lifting me up easily and walking us toward the bed.

When we reach it, he stops and sets me on my feet again, my heart still pounding from the close contact with his bare skin, the press of his cock along the smooth skin of my stomach.

"Turn around," he murmurs, and I suppress a little shiver of excitement and do as I'm told.

He wraps something soft around my face, blocking my sight. His shirt, I realize, as he ties it behind my head, blindfolding me. His hands slide down my back, caressing me, reaching down to cup my ass and squeeze gently, massaging my cheeks as he stands behind me, close enough that I can feel the heat radiating from his skin.

"Climb onto the bed, Sasha," he says.

I drop forward onto my knees, and crawl a

198

few paces along the bed, until I'm kneeling facing away from him. I feel the weight of the mattress shift under me as he climbs on behind me and positions himself at my rear, his hands still on my ass, as though he can't get enough of me, can't stop touching me.

I fucking love that.

"I'm going to fuck you now, Sasha," he murmurs, even as he traces his cock along the backs of my thighs, then between my legs, with slow strokes, letting me feel every inch of him, the velvety smooth skin over his hard shaft turning me on.

"Please fucking do," I manage to say, distracted as I am. Then I lick my lips, turn my head a little so he can see me smile, and add in my best sultry tone, "Master."

"You like that, don't you?" I can hear the answering grin in his voice. "You like submitting to me. Knowing that you're mine. Knowing I'm going to do what I want with you."

"I do, Master."

"Good. Because I intend to keep having my way with you, Sasha." He presses his cock between my thighs, right along the length of my slit. I'm soaked already, and he chuckles a little as he notices this, sliding his cock back and forth along my slit to coat himself in my juices. "I'm going to have my way with you for a long, long time."

I spread my legs a little to grant him better access, breath coming hard and fast, my heart racing. But he keeps going slow, so slow it's agonizing, almost torture—he takes his time parting my ass cheeks with his hands, squeezing hard enough to leave marks, and tracing his cock along my lips, one after the other.

"Fuck," I hiss, when he's still teasing me far too long later.

He laughs again. "Anxious, little slave?"

"Fuck yes I am." I bite my lip, frustrated.

"You want me to fuck you properly now?" He slides a hand between my legs and fingers my clit, rolling it gently between his thumb and his forefinger, adding just enough pressure to set off fireworks in my veins.

I can only nod.

Without warning, he thrusts his cock into me, deep and fast. I cry out with pleasure, feeling him stretch my walls, fill me completely. He grabs my hips and pulls me back against him, his cock spearing deep into my pussy.

I fall forward, my forehead pressed into the bed as he draws back out of me, then thrusts back in, faster this time. This angle makes his cock feel like it's even bigger, pushing in deeper. I've never felt so full before, and it's driving me wild. I try to thrust back against him, but Grant holds my hips tight, pinning me in place as he starts to rock back and forth, building momentum.

"You like that? You like my fat cock inside your pussy?"

I moan with want, bucking against him as he starts to fuck me faster.

"Tell me how much you like my cock inside you, Sasha. Tell me what it feels like."

I bite my lip to draw my brain back into itself, because otherwise it's too hard to get lost in the sensation. Still, forming words is difficult when he's doing this to me, making me crazy with lust. I swallow hard and force myself to think around the swell of pleasure growing deep in my belly. "It… feels like you fill every inch of me," I manage, my breath coming harder, faster, as he continues to fuck me. "Your cock is so fucking big and hard and… *fuck,*" I cry out as he thrusts into me again, his balls slapping against my clit at this angle. "I love feeling you inside me, stretching me out, making me ache with want. I love it when you come in me."

"You like that? You like when I pump my cum into your tight little pussy, fill you with my seed?"

I moan again. "Fuck yes I do."

He laughs once, softly, and slows in his pounding for a moment, hands sliding up my sides

202

to cup my breasts, his thumb and forefinger teasing at my hardened nipples. Rolling them until I gasp from the sensation. "I thought you wanted me to come in your mouth this time, City Girl. You're going to have to make up your mind."

"I…"

Damn. I bite my lip. I do want to taste him. But it felt so good when he came in me last night— I'd forgotten what that felt like, fucking like this. Raw, as he put it.

Grant doesn't wait for me to answer. He keeps going, picking up the pace, fucking me on all fours. At the same time, he reaches between my legs with his free hand and presses his thumb to my clit. I cry out, unable to contain it. My clit is already aching for release, turned on as hell from sucking his cock. It feels swollen, like ripe fruit between my thighs begging for him to pluck it.

"Fuck," I hiss, as the building pleasure distracts me.

"Going to have to decide soon," he says,

stroking my clit in time with his thrusts now, driving me wild. His cock is so thick that it presses against my inner walls, and with each thrust, his head grazes my G-spot, makes my pussy clench tight and my body quiver as I build toward an orgasm.

He stops stroking me, right as I'm nearing the edge, and I shout in protest.

"Tell me where you want me to come, and then you can come," Grant says, his voice steady, infuriatingly so, as he continues to fuck me at the same steady, grinding pace.

"My mouth," I gasp. "I want you to come in my mouth."

His finger returns to my clit, and I scream wordlessly as the orgasm hits me almost instantly. My pussy tightens, convulses around his cock, and he drives into me faster, his muscles taut, his hands hard on my hips, fucking me as I finish, his cock sliding over my G-spot again and again to keep me at my peak.

Finally, I sink toward the sheets, gasping. But without warning, Grant pulls out of me. My pussy tightens again, feeling empty without him. He doesn't give me time to think about it, though, as he rolls me over on the bed. The blindfold falls off, but I don't care—I'm grateful for the sight of him above me, his eyes dark with lust, his mouth a hard line as he holds his cock erect between us, wet with my juices.

"Suck my cock clean, Sasha," he growls, and I scramble upright to obey him, all too eager.

The taste of myself mixed with him is intoxicating. I lick and suck at his tip, but I don't have much time. He grabs my head with both hands, pulls me closer, his cock sliding deeper into my throat as he comes with a loud cry, guttural and animal with lust. I swallow hard, taking as much of him as I can, savoring his flavor, his taste, the white-hot rush of him.

When he finally pulls back, his hands trembling, I sit up and grab his face, pull him to me in another deep kiss. His tongue slips into my mouth again, and I know he can taste our flavors too, the combination of us, the scent of our sex heavy in the air.

When we part, we're both breathing hard, our faces flushed, bodies damp with sweat. And we're both grinning like idiots.

"Fuck," I manage, as I sit back on the bed, still quivering, my pussy sensitive and pleasantly sore.

"You can say that again," Grant murmurs. He draws me up to my feet beside him and wraps his arms around me for a long moment. I lean into him, savor the feeling of his strong arms around me, the scent of his body, and the tingle in my limbs from the orgasm.

"I'll be your slave any day," I murmur into his chest, and he laughs softly, then taps my chin. Tilts my head back and leans down to kiss me once more, soft and slow this time.

"Good," he says softly against my lips.

"Because I'm not ready to let you go just yet…"

Chapter 9

Sasha Bluebell

The next morning, I wake up in Grant's arms. It's still dark outside—even Mr. Early Bird isn't up yet. But part of him is. I realize what prodded me awake, and I grin and arch my back a little to grind my hips against his, against the hard press of his boner I can already feel digging into the small of my back.

Grant moans softly in his sleep, and I rotate my hips again, teasing.

His hand slides around my waist, and he pulls me against him, his lips teasing along my neck. "That's certainly one way to wake up a man," he murmurs, his other hand sliding down my waist, around my front. He flattens his palm against my stomach and lowers his hand toward my bare pussy. We both slept naked last night, since we fucked again the minute we got home from the Johnsons' party.

I grin and wriggle my hips again. "Is that so?"

"Mm... Playing with fire there," he whispers. "Keep doing that, and I might have to show you a thing or two about what happens to naughty little girls who wake me up."

"Is that so?" I glance over my shoulder, a challenge flaring in my eyes. "Maybe you'll just have to explain it to me, then, Mr. Werther."

"Gladly," he murmurs, nipping at my earlobe lightly. I gasp, but his bite quickly shifts into a soft, caressing lick, then a kiss, as he works his way down the side of my neck.

"Mm... For punishment, this isn't so bad," I whisper as he wraps his arms around me and pulls my body against his possessively. His cock presses against the backs of my thighs, and I'm getting wet already just feeling him there, so close to my pussy, so hard with desire for me. "I might have to wake you up more often."

I can feel him smile against the nape of my neck, a motion that sends another cascade of shivers trickling down my spine. "Uh oh. She's discovered my motive."

I laugh, and turn to catch his eye. But he presses his mouth to mine in a long, slow kiss, and I'm distracted from whatever I was going to say. My lips part, and his tongue traces along mine, tentative, gentle. At the same time, his hand slides from my hip to my thighs, and gently draws my upper leg up, parting my thighs enough that his cock can slide between them, thick and meaty between my legs. I sigh into his mouth, and he draws back far enough to look at me, that same hungry look in his eye. Only this time it's softer, sweeter. He looks at me like he can't believe I'm here.

I know the feeling. I'm not sure what I expected when I came home to the farm, but it definitely wasn't this. It wasn't him.

Grant Werther came out of nowhere.

His cock parts my pussy lips, and I arch my hips back against him to grant him easier access. At the same time, he reaches down to circle his fingertips across my mound, slowly increasing pressure with every circulation, making my clit tingle with pleasure. It doesn't take long before I'm breathing faster, my body quivering at his touch. Only then does he arch his hips forward, slide his cock straight up to my entrance.

Fuck, I'm already so wet for him.

"God you are perfect, Sasha," he murmurs softly, those eyes still fixed on mine, holding me in place, unable to look away.

I can't look away from him—but I don't *want* to, either. I want to drink in that look in his eyes over and over, as long as I can.

He pushes his hips forward in one slow, smooth motion, and the tip of his cock spreads my lips. Inches into my pussy, centimeter by torturous centimeter. I gasp softly, wriggling against him, trying to push him deeper, faster.

"Always so impatient," he scolds, a hint of a smile on his mouth. He's still holding me against him, the little spoon to his bigger one, and I love this feeling, being completely enfolded in his body, even as his thick cock begins to fill me up.

"What can I say?" I smile back, arching a brow. "I like having your big cock inside me, Country Man."

"Addicted already, City Girl?" He smirks, and with that, thrusts the rest of the way into me all at once, one swift hard motion.

I cry out with pleasure, my hands fisting in the sheets beside us.

"I'll take that as a yes," he replies, laughing softly, as he begins to draw out of me again.

"You do have a great cock, I'll grant you that," I manage, recovering enough to arc my hips back, angling toward him.

He thrusts into me again, and lets out a soft, faint groan. "Your pussy is fairly addictive too, City Girl." He pulls out, and now we both thrust together, our breaths coming shorter as we move in sync. "So fucking tight. And you're always so wet for me…"

"Sounds like we're both addicted," I murmur, grinning, as we start to thrust in sync now, his cock spreading the walls of my pussy wide as he fills me again and again.

"Sounds like," he agrees softly, and then I lose track of his voice, lost instead in the feeling of his hands exploring me—one toying with my clit, the other wrapped tight around my waist—and his cock thrusting inside me.

I lose track of everything. The farm, the bedroom, the outside world. The whole world narrows until it's just me and Grant and everything between us.

We both come together, him stroking me right up to the edge of my climax before his cock dragging along my front wall, right over my G-spot, sends me over the brink. He finishes at the same time, growling with lust as he pulls my hips back hard against his, pumping every ounce of his cum into me. I tighten my pussy, clench hard around him to milk every last drop, loving the sensation, the sheer animal lust of it.

We collapse against the sheets together, tangled up, spent, and only then does dawn hint at the curtains, painting them a pale pink. A reminder of another day dawning. Another day less that we have together.

I push up out of bed, mostly to distract myself from how nice it feels to lie there in his arms. I can't get too comfortable. This is temporary, all of it. I can enjoy it while it lasts, but I can't let myself relax too much.

I can't start to fall for him. Not when he's... who he is. A country man, a farm boy, a representative of everything I left behind. Everything I thought I was over in life.

I pad into the shower alone, leaving him on the bed. He watches me go, his eyes dark, unreadable, and I wonder if he's thinking the same thing. He must be. He knows this can't last, too.

Still. We can enjoy it while it does.

That's what I tell myself as I plunge my head under the shower tap and try to block out the rushing sound in my ears. The sound of something like regret.

That night, after dinner, Grant stops me as I stand up to do the dishes.

"It's my turn," I protest, but he ignores that and clasps my hand instead. Leads me out back. I laugh and tug at his grip. "Where are we going?"

"You'll see," is his only reply. I'm learning that my country man likes to do that—make mysterious promises.

I have to admit, he's lived up to all of them so far. So even though I roll my eyes and sigh, I do relax and let him lead me.

We pad across the grass together, barefoot.

That tickles something at the back of my mind, a distant memory. Doing this before. Tiptoeing through this dewy grass, feeling the mud squish between my toes and tickle the soles of my feet. For some reason, in my memory, it seems like Grant was there. Though of course, I know he can't have been. I remember him from high school now, vaguely—the big handsome guy who hung out with the jocks. We didn't really cross paths much, even though our parents were friends.

Well, Mama, anyway, was friends with his parents. As for Dad...

I shake that thought off the way I always do. Douse those memories in kerosene and light the mental match. I don't need to go down that road. Too much could catch fire.

I force myself back to the present, to the Grant who's here with me now. The Grant I never knew back then. The one I wished I'd known better, if he was anything like the man he is now. Maybe if we'd been better friends in school, I wouldn't have written this whole town off as useless.

He leads me out into the fields. We climb over the fence together, he lifts me up easily while I swing my legs over the posts. Then, hand in hand once more, we tiptoe through the fallows, over the now-empty fields that will one day—probably not until next year though—hold crops again. These fields will grow food, sustain life. Be productive in a real, tangible way. The kind of productivity that's easy to wrap your head around. You get your hands dirty, dig in this soil, and in turn it feeds you.

At the core of it, that's what life is really about. All the stuff I get up to back at home in the city, that's all a kind of crazy distillation of this. It's fun, but it's not quite as... *real*, somehow.

It's not simple, anyway. It's not easy to understand. It's not feeding yourself off the fruits of your labor—except maybe metaphorically, with all the money I make from being a desk jockey, running errands and playing glorified secretary. I feel like I've been lost behind a computer screen for the last few years, and only now am I waking up to it. Remembering what life used to be like a million years ago... before.

Before I let the stress get to me, start dictating my life. Before I let other people control everything—my schedule, my plans, my happiness.

Back when things, just like life on this farm, were simpler.

"You doing okay, City Girl?" Grant asks, tugging on my hand a little. I realize I've been lagging behind him, my feet slowing as I tilt my head back to take in the sky, the stars, the endless expanse above us.

I shake myself and jog a few steps to catch up with him. "Doing just fine," I say.

"Not too dirty and messy for you?" he asks. I know he's joking now. He's seen how down and dirty I'm willing to get.

In more ways than one.

"Never," I promise, and he laughs softly.

Then we round the corner, past the fields,

toward the trees that edge the borderline of Mama's property, and I gasp.

I don't know how he set this up. He must have taken a while, snuck out in between projects back at the house somehow. My eyes widen, taking it in. He's built a whole tent out here—not a simple pitch tent either, but a big billowing thing made of silk, taller than both of us, with open sides. In the center is a little fire pit, and there is a tray, with all the ingredients for s'mores arranged on it. Not to mention, a little bucket of ice with a bottle of wine cooling in it.

"I know you're used to the finer things in life," he's saying. "I just wanted to point out that you don't have to be fancy to know how to pamper someone properly."

I laugh, not sure what to say. Not sure what this feeling is beating in my chest, as he kneels down on the blanket he's laid out as the base of the tent and sets about building up the fire.

The peak of the tent stands out stark white

against the night sky, stars twinkling all across the background. It looks like something out of a movie or a painting. It looks fake, all of this. Too pretty to be real. Especially when he gets the fire going and beckons me down to his side.

I drop down beside him, snuggle in next to him as we listen to crickets in the distance. Fireflies wink here and there over the field, and we hear the soft hoots of owls, the distant reverberations of frogs somewhere in the forest, where there's a little stream that runs past the property. I breathe in deep, savoring the scent of the fire crackling away merrily at our feet, mingled with the cool, crisp fall air, so fresh that I can't believe I ever thought I could breathe properly at home. You never notice things like that—stale, muggy, smog-choked air—until you're away from it. Until real fresh air fills your lungs, and suddenly you realize what you've been missing.

It's not just the air I've been missing, I realize.

Grant hands me a stick, a marshmallow already speared on its tip, and I grin at him. Huddled up beside him, wrapped in the blanket that he tugs up over our knees, I set about toasting this marshmallow to perfection. He's a burner—he just sets his on fire, blows it out a few times, and calls it a day. Me, I like to slowly toast it. Get all the sides evenly browned before I slide it off the stick onto the chocolate-covered graham crackers to make the sandwich.

"You're such a perfectionist," he accuses me, and I elbow him, eying his attempts.

"You're so lazy," I counter.

"Not lazy." He takes a huge bite, chases it with a sip of the wine he's poured for us both. "Just practical. I get things done, you know."

I laugh. "I've noticed. You're making good headway back at the house."

"Can't say you haven't been a big help, City Girl. Despite appearances."

I snort and roll my eyes. "What, like I can't

do work just because I dress fancy?"

"You can't blame me for making assumptions."

"Sure I can. Why are you so biased against city people anyway?"

"Why are you so biased against everyone in this town?" He raises an eyebrow.

I bite my lip. Fair. "They never liked me," I reply, shaking my head.

"That so?"

"I mean... I don't know. I was never super close with anyone here."

"So that's their fault then?"

I laugh. "No. I just didn't jive. I wasn't built for this life."

"You seem to be enjoying yourself this week," he points out.

I heave a deep sigh, leaning back against his side, my eyes on the open sides of the tent. Out beyond the tent, the fireflies continue to flit across the field and along the edge of the forest, their lights

222

winking like tiny stars against the dark grass. "I like it here, sure. It's just… I don't know."

For once, he just waits me out in silence.

I draw in a deep breath as I try to find the words to explain. "I had to get away," I finally say. "To prove to myself that I could. To prove I wouldn't get stuck here."

"Is that really such a bad fate? Being stuck here?"

I laugh again, faintly. When we're sitting out here in this field, surrounded by nature, by magic almost, sharing these s'mores and wine, after a long hard day that left my muscles aching pleasantly— not to mention a long night before that of sex that left me feeling happier and more fulfilled than I have in ages… No. I have to admit, it's not. "I suppose I can think of worse fates," I murmur finally.

We lapse into silence for a while, the only sound the crackling of the fire. Then Grant sets up another marshmallow, and we go back to playfully bickering about the proper way to roast them and which one of us is committing a cardinal sin by not putting the right amount of chocolate on the graham crackers first (clearly him, because you need two bars of chocolate to make a proper s'more).

In retribution, or maybe just to prove his point, he smears some of the chocolate across my face, and then it's war. I rub some into his beard, and he tackles me across the tent. Pins me underneath him, both of us panting with effort as I struggle to get free.

"No use," he tells me, those dark eyes of his going serious now. "You're all mine now, City Girl. There's no escaping."

I wriggle beneath him, arching up to press my hips against his. I can already see the bulge forming in his jeans, impossible to satiate as he is. That's fine by me. I can't get enough of him either. "How terrible," I say, grinning. "Trapped by a Country Man."

"You're enjoying this too much," he scolds.

I smirk. "Not my fault you make getting caught so enjoyable."

"What can I say? I like capturing city girls." He reaches down to grab the hem of my T-shirt and tugs it up my body slowly. "Though I must say, this outfit screams country to me. Are you forgetting yourself down here on the farm?"

"Maybe." I raise my hips, lifting my body off the ground a little to balance on my shoulders and let him slide my shirt up higher, up above my bra, the lace peeking out now. "Or maybe I'm just remembering myself. Told you I was born as country as you are, didn't I?"

"You did mention that." His dark eyes catch mine, a smirk in them. "I might even be starting to believe you."

I huff in faux indignation, even as he tugs my shirt the rest of the way off and tosses it down beside us. With my hands freed, while his are occupied, I reach up for his shirt too. I tug it off and run my fingertips over the stark outline of his muscles, tracing his pecs, his flat abs, then the deep V at his groin, pointing straight down to where I really want to reach.

Before I can slip my hands down his jeans, though, he catches my wrists and lifts my hands again. He folds both of my wrists easily into one hand and pins it over my head, clicking his tongue as he leans down to kiss my neck, my chest, his tongue flicking into the hollow at the base of my clavicle.

"Not so fast, impatient girl," he murmurs. "I plan to take my time tonight."

He reaches under me and unhooks my bra, then pushes that aside, his mouth still on my chest. He kisses down the center of my chest, then trails his tongue along the underside of each of my breasts, one after the other. His other hand kneads my opposite breast, his palms rough against my soft, smooth skin. My nipples start to harden, especially when he wraps his mouth around one of my breasts and trails the flat plane of his tongue across my nipple in one long, slow lick. Then he pulls back a little to circle the tip of his tongue around my areola, teasing, and I gasp faintly, arching up into him. He moans against my skin, and I sigh with pleasure at the vibrations that reverberate throughout my whole body.

He turns to minister to my other nipple, doing the same thing, tonguing along the top and bottom of my breast before he circles in on my nipple, sucking it hard into his mouth and gently rolling it between his teeth until I gasp and twist under him. With his hand, he rolls my other nipple between his thumb and forefinger, keeping it hard, tugging gently, not enough to hurt, just enough to make the pleasant sensation fire through all my nerves, and I moan loudly.

Only when both of my nipples are rock hard and aching from the attention does he begin to trail his tongue down my abs. He kisses, nips and licks his way to my navel, then dips his tongue inside, sending a shock of sensation all the way down to my toes.

My legs drop flat under him as he reaches down to undo my jean shorts with one hand, the other still holding my wrists pinned. I struggle slightly against him, wanting to reach for his jeans too, wanting to reciprocate, but he peers up at me, those dark eyes commanding.

"Relax, Sasha," he murmurs. "You'll get your turn." Then he smirks and shoves my shorts down my hips, bending down to kiss the sensitive skin between my navel and the top of my mound, grinning at the way that makes me shiver. "Right now, it's my turn to drive you wild."

I force myself to take his advice. To lie back and let myself go. He releases my wrists, and I don't let myself reach for him. I only push myself up a little, high enough to look down and watch him as he peels off my shorts, then kisses my mound through the thin fabric of my panties. His lips are white-hot against my skin, and my whole body fires with want. I want—no, I *need* him. But at the same time, I don't want this moment to end.

So I force my usual impatient nature to quiet.

Grant bites my inner thigh gently, just hard enough that I jump and gasp again. He loves making me do that, the bastard.

"Sensitive City Girl," he points out.

"Only when you make me that way, Country Man," I murmur.

This time when he bites down, it's through the fabric of my panties. Then he leans his head up, draws back just far enough to keep the fabric between his teeth, and pushes himself backwards, tugging my panties with them, using only his teeth.

I catch my breath. *Fuck*, he's hot. Especially now, looking up at me with blatant, sheer desire in his gaze.

I lift my hips up enough to let him pull my panties down, and he inhales sharply as he does, drawing them down to my knees and leaving them tangled there.

"Wet for me already," he points out, grinning. "This is becoming a habit."

You're becoming a habit, I almost say. But I swallow those words at the last moment, think better of it. Because he isn't a habit. He *can't* be.

His tongue distracts me from any more thoughts along those lines, though, when he licks his way up my inner thigh, making my whole body go tense and loose at once. He trails his tongue up slowly, first up one thigh then the other, wet and hot against my skin. When he lifts his head to smile up at me, a dark, mischievous grin on his face, my skin feels extra cool in the evening air, the coolness compounding with the heat of his hands on my stomach, tracing my thighs. The contrast is delicious, even more so when he bends to lick directly across my mound, pressing hard enough with his tongue that I can feel the pressure all the way into my clit.

He pushes my thighs apart in one swift motion, his hands digging into the plump flesh of my thighs, holding me down as he bends down to trail his tongue along my outer lips, one after the other.

"Fuck you taste incredible," he murmurs in between licks, before he parts my lips with two fingers and runs his tongue up my slit, all the way from the back to the front, licking up my juices which have already gathered there.

My head falls back against the soft blankets, my eyes fixed on the billowing ceiling of the tent as I moan, long and loud.

"I love this sexy, tight pussy," Grant whispers, and his breath feels even hotter against my wet skin. He leans in to press his tongue between my lips again, pressing right against the entrance of my pussy, and I groan, my hips rising of their own accord. With one hand, he presses them back down to the blanket, and with one last push, his tongue slides into my pussy.

Fuck. He feels incredible. My vision goes blurry, hazy, as I lose focus, distracted by him. He tongues each of my walls at a time, one after the other, as he inches his tongue deeper. When he's speared his tongue as deep inside me as it will go, he curls it up and drags it down my front inner wall, a practiced motion that makes my clit throb and my pussy feel tight and wet with desire.

He flattens his tongue to a blade and draws it out of my pussy, up over my clit, licking it once, hard. My hips jerk from the sudden flood of sensation, and I can't control the sounds that are coming out of me anymore, the low, desperate moans.

He keeps going, alternating between delving his tongue into my pussy and then drawing it out to lick my clit over and over, until it's driving me wild, my whole body shaking and my hips bucking against his mouth.

Then, out of nowhere, he sits up.

I gasp, this time in protest, and reach for his head, trying to pull him back.

He smirks and catches both my hands.

Kisses my palms one after another as he watches me. "You want me to keep going?" he asks.

"Yes," I pant.

"How badly?" he asks.

I scowl, frustrated. "I…"

"Beg me to make you come, Sasha. Beg me to lick you until you can't stand it, until you scream so loud you wake up everyone for miles around."

Damn him. I press my lips together, frustrated.

He lifts an eyebrow, waiting.

I blow out a sharp breath of air. "Please, Grant."

"Please what?" he taunts, tilting his head with a smirk.

"Please… Make me come."

"How do you want me to make you come, Sasha?"

"I want you…" I lick my lips, swallowing hard. "I want you to lick my pussy. I want you to tongue me until I can't stand it."

His smile widens. "Your wish is my command." He ducks between my thighs again, and I bury my hands in his hair as he pushes his tongue straight into my pussy once more, circling it inside me.

When he pulls his tongue out to pay attention to my clit, I pant louder, my breath coming hard and fast as I arch up to press my pussy closer to his mouth. At the same time I tighten my fists in his hair, pull him against me as his tongue laps across me again and again, over and over, until I can't stand it, the pressure is building so high it'll drive me mad.

"I'm going to come," I cry out faintly, trying to catch my breath. "Fuck, Grant, don't stop, I'm going to come…"

He circles his tongue right over my clit, sensing exactly what I need. That motion is enough to send me over the edge, and I scream with pleasure as the orgasm hits me. It rockets through my body, echoing all the way down to my toes and my fingertips, flooding my brain with ecstasy.

My vision turns to blurry sparks, and my body shakes from the force of it, my pussy convulsing.

Grant, for his part, doesn't stop. He just leans back a little and slides one finger into me, even as my pussy clamps down tightly around him. He curls it inside me, drags his finger along my front wall with practiced motions, finding my G-spot easily. He adds a second finger, then leans down to tongue my clit again at the same time, and I cry out once more, my voice harsh from overuse.

Fuck, I think, or maybe scream, I'm not sure. His touch keeps the sensation going, keeps my body hovering right there on the brink, as I brace for an aftershock. But with his fingers inside me, pressing against my G-spot, stroking in and out, filling me, and his tongue still lashing across my clit again and again, unrelenting, the second orgasm hits harder than the first. My hips buck, and I can hardly catch my breath, my whole body shaking hard.

He finally draws his fingers out of me, only when my hips sag back against the blanket and my eyes drift closed, the sheer force of that orgasm making me relaxed, stunned. He sits upright and I peer down to watch him licking his fingers clean, one at a time, eyes focused on mine.

But if anything, all those orgasms did was make me hungrier for him. Hungry to have him fill me completely, in the way only his cock can do.

I reach up for him eagerly, and he falls across me on all fours as I fumble with the button of his jeans. He's rock hard underneath, and it only takes a moment for me to shove his jeans down, his boxers after them, until his cock springs free.

Now he's the impatient one.

"Fuck, Sasha." He grabs my legs and spreads them wide, kneeling between. I arch up to wrap my thighs around his waist, as he lines up his cock with my soaking wet entrance. "You are so. Fucking. Perfect," he murmurs as he stares into my eyes, slowly, slowly pressing into me.

He feels incredible. My pussy is already sensitive from the double orgasm, and the feeling of his cock spreading me, stretching me to my limit, drives me wild. I tighten my legs around his waist with every inch he pushes into me, and when he's finally completely inside me, I wrap my arms around his shoulders too, hold him there inside me for a moment, just savoring the feeling of his cock, his body, *him*, here with me.

"Fuck you feel so fucking incredible," he murmurs.

"I fucking love it when you fill me up," I gasp. "I can't get enough…"

"Good." Those dark eyes latch onto mine. I could stare into his eyes forever and never get tired of this look he gives me. Like he cannot drink me in long enough. Like he's almost scared of what he feels for me.

I know the feeling. I am too.

"Neither can I," he admits. Then he's drawing back, out of me, and I gasp a little in protest. But it doesn't last long—he thrusts back inside me a moment later, and I buck up against him, eager, insatiable.

Grant starts to rock back and forth, thrusting into me slowly at first, but building momentum. I meet him thrust for thrust, arcing my hips to push up against his with every moment. Before long, we're both gasping, clinging to one another, my nails digging into his back and his hands so tight on my hip I know he'll leave marks tomorrow. I don't care. I want those marks. Evidence of how much he wants me—how much I cause him to lose control.

Before long we're both thrusting as hard as we can, fucking hard and fast, my whole body alight with pleasure, on fire for him. Sensitive as I am, it doesn't take me long to build back up to the edge, my clit throbbing with the force of the last two orgasms still.

Grant unhooks my legs from around him, flings them up over his shoulders and keeps fucking me, his cock dragging right over my G-spot now, the head rubbing along it until I cry aloud and feel my toes curl, my nerves catching fire with another orgasm.

"Fuck. Sasha... I'm..."

Grant is lost now, driving into me, all animal now. Before long, I sense him nearing his peak, and I tighten my pussy as much as I can, clenching hard around him. He moans aloud when I do that, and I feel his cock tense and jump inside me as he comes, squirting deep inside me, coating my insides with his hot cum. It feels white hot inside my pussy, like a balm after all the hard fucking.

When he pulls out of me, we both laugh softly at the hot rush that trickles down my leg, puddling on the blanket beneath me.

Grant collapses beside me, still breathing hard. "That..."

"Was incredible," I finish, curling against him. He's slick with sweat, but then, so am I. Our skin cools together in the night air, and we lie there beside the slowly dying fire, soaked in our sweat, the scent of sex mingling with the smells of the outdoors and the fields and the wild, until we're both shivering. Only then, reluctantly, do we sit up and reach for our clothes.

But Grant stops me before I tug mine back on, a spark in his eyes. "Why redress?" he asks with a shrug. "If we need to go shower anyway."

I laugh. Then lift my eyebrows, watching him. Why, indeed?

He douses the fire, and then, with our clothes tucked under our arms, hand-in-hand, we pad back across the fields. This time we're not just barefoot, we're completely naked. But there's something so freeing about it. About feeling the night air on my skin, the moonlight illuminating us, the bright stars overhead our only witnesses.

I could get used to this, I think as we reach the farmhouse again, and Grant opens the door for me, bows me inside with a wink, ever the gentleman.

That's the dangerous part. I could very, very

easily get used to this.

Chapter 10

Grant Werther

What is this girl doing to me? I've never felt like this before.

I thought I was going to go crazy at the Johnsons' party, watching her strutting around in that sexy, tight little dress. And when I won the bet after we played pool, it took every ounce of self-restraint I had not to bend her over the table and claim her right there, onlookers be damned.

We've spent the last two days since the party doing nothing but fucking. Well, working on the house, in between. But those hours tend to fly past in a daze, with half my mind focused on the next time I'll get to strip her down and take my time making her come again and again. I barely even notice the work I'm doing, because I'm so focused on thinking about her tight little ass, her sexy breasts and her perfect pussy. The way her voice goes throaty and sultry when she's trying to turn me on (which really doesn't take much). The way she gasps when she comes, or how her pussy always contracts around my cock when her orgasm hits with my dick balls-deep inside her.

Fuck. I'm getting hard now just thinking about it, and I still have to finish this fence before nightfall. We're running short on days now. Short on days and time. Something I don't want to think about.

So I just keep focusing on the work. The work and Sasha's perfect body.

Not to mention our conversations. Over dinner every night, she tells me about everything she accomplished during the day, her eyes bright with excitement. She doesn't even notice it. She doesn't hear the way she's enjoying this, getting down and dirty, putting some callouses on those smooth, sexy city hands of hers.

At night, we lie side-by-side out in the yard, counting stars—or ignoring the stars when we lose ourselves in each other more often than not. But just last night, after we fucked hard in the grass, covering ourselves in dew, I pulled her onto my chest to watch the night sky, and she sighed, cuddling into me.

"I feel more relaxed right now than I have in years," she whispered, and I held her tighter. Willed her to hear her own words. To realize what they mean.

But she doesn't.

This morning over breakfast, she popped in with a cheery smile, talking about what a nice vacation this has been. A great break from the work she's going to have to go back and slog through as soon as we're done. She went on a twenty minute rant about work, and I didn't say a word, just buried my face in my cereal bowl, because how am I supposed to respond to that?

You can't exactly say *wake up and smell the country-baked bread, Sasha, you're not meant for city life*. You can't exactly tell somebody that they're glowing in a way they weren't just days ago. You can't tell someone what to do in their life, even when you know what's right for them, when you know they'd be happier if they listened to you.

You can't, because that's up to them. They need to figure out their own lives. Make their own calls.

Even if it kills you to watch.

"Lunch?" Sasha calls from the house, and I dust off my palms, glance over my shoulder at her. She's still wearing those jean shorts. She loves how wild they drive me. Loves positioning herself right in front of me to work, so I'm stuck staring at that juicy, pert little ass until I can't take it anymore and I give up on work and go to peel those jean shorts off.

But I shake off that urge right now. I'm too annoyed after this morning.

"I'm good," I call, and turn back to the fence. I figure that'll be the end of it until I hear the now familiar sound of bare feet padding across the grass.

"What's up with you?" a voice asks at my elbow. I've come to recognize that tone of hers by now. The exasperated one. The one she turns on when I don't want to talk—but she does.

"Don't know what you mean," I reply, hefting the post holer into position and stomping it into the muddy grass. It's shocking how fast the holes left by the fallen posts of this fence filled up. Nature has a way of claiming anything left alone long enough. And God knows this poor farm was left to its own devices for far too long.

Thanks to Sasha, I remind myself. Thanks to the runaway daughter nobody ever thought we'd see around here again. Thanks to the runaway I'm being idiotic enough to start falling for.

No. I'm not falling. I'm just… Enjoying this ride.

"You've been weird all day," she says. "You skipped breakfast, you don't want lunch either?"

"I'm not hungry." I draw up the holer and

squint down into the hole its left behind in the ground. A perfect square-peg hole, just big enough for the new fence post. Looks deep enough, too, at last, so I bend down to pick up the post and start to position it in the hole.

"You aren't talking to me either." She crosses her arms and bends into my field of view while I fiddle with the fence. Her foot starts tapping, in a nervous, energetic way that frays my already spent nerves.

"I'm a bit busy," I point out. But she's clearly not going to let this drop, so I straighten and wipe my sweaty hair back from my brow, squinting at her in the midday sun. The fence is almost finished. Two more posts, then I just need to finish stringing the wire along it, and it's ready.

The house is looking miles better too. The roof is done. The gardens are weeded and re-seeded with attractive plants. The front gate has been oiled and straightened on its hinges. The electrical wiring has been finished inside, the rooms all repainted, cleaned and tidied. It's still not a state-of-the-art modern cabin, but it was never going to be that.

It's back to what it always was, at least. Cozy. Comfortable. Neat. A real home. The kind of home someone could live in.

The kind of home I feel like we've been living in for the past week. We haven't really, I know. We're just guests. But... It doesn't feel like that. Not while I'm right here in the middle of it.

None of this feels temporary. Not even the way Sasha is glaring at me right now, head cocked, those shrewd green eyes of hers flashing. She knows that something's bothering me, and she's not going to let up about it—like anyone in a relationship wouldn't.

Except this isn't a relationship. She's about to turn tail and run, in less than two days, as soon as we officially declare this farm ready for sale.

"Seriously, Grant," she says, and I can't help it. I relent a little, relax at the sound of my name on her perfect, smooth, so-fucking-kissable lips. "Tell me what's wrong. Please."

"Farm's looking great," I say instead, squinting past her at the fields. We haven't gotten around to seeding those yet, but we've tilled them. They're almost in workable order. Too late in the season for any produce this year, but next spring they'll be ripe for the planting. For whatever lucky owner wants to come and try their luck at growing anything out here.

A frown line appears on her brow. But she follows my gaze nonetheless, and studies the place alongside me. "We'll be finished by tomorrow or the next day, don't you think?" she agrees softly.

"Easily. Maybe sooner if we hustle on the fence and the back garden."

Now it's her turn to sigh and run her hands through her hair. She stretches, and I can't help it— my gaze drops to trace her curves. The tug of her breasts under her tight T-shirt, the way her flat belly peeks out between the hem of that shirt and the edge of her tiny, sexy little jean shorts.

"I never thought it would look this good this fast," she admits, her voice low. "When I first pulled up here..." She laughs and shakes her head a little.

I smirk. "You were very concerned, I seem to recall. About the fence, the house, the tire swing..."

She snorts. "Well. There's one thing we still need to fix. That tire swing is definitely a death-trap."

"I don't know about that," I counter, raising an eyebrow. "It always was sturdy." There it is again. The reminder that she doesn't even remember. The two of us taking turns on that swing, me pushing her so high she screamed. Her trying and failing to push me hard enough to get any momentum at all. Us standing on opposite sides, winding it up and letting go so it spun, and pulled us apart, both of us shrieking, hanging onto the rope for dear life as it spun.

"I bet we'll get a lot more than you first

expected," Sasha says, eyes still on the property. Because of course. That's all she sees in this place. Future money. A burden to offload on someone else.

"I'd reckon so," I reply, my tone carefully, painfully neutral.

"What do you plan to do with your share?" she asks, head tilted. Oblivious to what she's doing. To how I'm feeling.

"Don't know."

She turns to look at me at last, frowning, head tilted in concern. "You don't know? It'll be a decent chunk of money. You must have some plans for it."

I wanted this farm. I wanted to be the one to take it, turn it back into what it used to be in its heyday. Or at least turn enough profit to keep going, to build a life here. A life for me, and...

It doesn't matter.

"You know me. I'm just a simple country man," I mutter. "Don't have any big lofty plans in life."

"I didn't mean that," Sasha protests. "I just meant... Surely you were thinking about... after..."

"Probably not as much as you. I'm sure you can't wait to get on home to your fancy new life. This all must seem way too simple for you. Boring and slow, just like all us townie folks."

"Grant, what—"

"That's fine, Sasha. You like what you like. You always have. You're exactly the same girl you used to be."

Her frown deepens now, creasing her forehead. "What are you talking about?"

"You don't even remember. That's the worst part. How can you be mad at someone for something they don't even remember doing?" I laugh and run my hand through my hair again. Then I tighten it into a fist, grimace, tug at my hair as I spin back toward the house.

"Of course I remember," she spits as she steps in my way, barring my path.

That throws me.

My brow furrows.

"I remember everything, Grant Werther. *You're* the one who didn't. You forgot that *of course* I know how to handle a hammer and climb a ladder —we built a whole tree house together. You forgot that we used to be friends before you got all high and mighty in high school, running with the jocks. You even forgot me—when I got here all you talked about was my mama and me leaving town. Like you didn't even remember those summers."

I'm staring at her, wide-eyed. *She never said...*

She shoves past me, shoulder colliding with mine. "But you're right," she says, angrily. "I can't wait to get home to my fancy life. Where I matter, where people give a damn about me."

She storms past me into the house.

It's too much. "Fine," I call after her. "Then you can go on back now, Sasha. I'll take care of the rest of this. Sell your share for you, and mail you the check. That's all you really want, isn't it? Go on home and leave the dirty work to me."

I don't look back to see if that blow landed. I don't stop walking until I'm at the back door of the house, wrenching it open, storming inside. I can't stand to look at her anymore. Those too-familiar green eyes, her face fallen in a sad expression. I can't take it.

She knew. All along she knew. She thought I didn't. What does that mean now?

It doesn't matter. She made clear just now what she intends to do about this—about us. I'm nothing more than a passing nostalgic fling to her. She's on her way back to the big city, and this time, I'll need to really forget about her, if I ever want to move on with my life.

Chapter 11

Sasha Bluebell

I stalk away across the fields, his words echoing through my mind.

You're exactly the same girl you used to be.

He acted like he didn't even recognize me. He *lied*. Pretended I was nothing more than some stranger whose property he owned half of, when all the time he knew everything. Now he expects me to, what? Suddenly feel nostalgic about him, this life, this place?

The fact that I do, a bit, isn't the point.

The girl who grew up here alongside Grant Werther is a completely different person. A past life. I've got a whole life waiting for me back home in the city, one I built myself. I don't need him or anyone.

You're exactly the same girl you used to be, he said. How can I be? I've run as far from her as I possibly can.

I pace along the fence he's been rebuilding. This part of the work he's done almost entirely himself. I reach out to run a hand along the wire that makes up most of the fence. My fingers dance across the wooden posts every few feet, tracing the rough material. A splinter pricks my finger at one point, and I draw it out with a sigh, dropping the pesky little sliver of wood to the grass at my feet.

Wish I could deal with all my problems that easily. Pluck them out and let them fall to the mud.

But this one, especially, is going to be hard to rid myself of.

So I try to do the one thing I really don't want to do.

I try to remember.

I start with the house itself. I have good memories there. Playing underfoot in the kitchen while Mama cooked. Running in and out of the living room, to… I grimace, rub my temples. But I force myself to relive that memory. Running in there to find Dad with a newspaper. Leaping onto the couch beside him, tugging at the paper. Making him sigh with exasperation, but then reach for me anyway, tug me onto his lap and ruffle my hair. He'd sit with me, let me read the paper with him, ignoring my childish attempts at pronouncing the big words in the news he always read.

Dad had wanderlust, Mama always said. He traveled for work at first, just weeklong trips here and there. I always cried when he left, but he never looked sad. He only looked sad when he came back.

That's what made him run in the end, she told me. He couldn't stand this life. Too country, too provincial. Too small.

He was never mean to us. Never seemed to hate us. Just… when he finally ran, his conscience didn't let him look back. He used to send me a letter once a year, on my birthday. They'd be filled with a whole lot of nothing. Just platitudes. "Miss you, hope you're doing well, thinking about you today." No details about where he was, what he was doing.

Why he left.

On my sixteenth birthday, the letters stopped coming.

On my eighteenth birthday, when I left for college, I burned the ones I had saved. I didn't need that reminder. No more than I needed him.

But I only ended up doing the same thing he did, I realize. I ran too, I left Mama behind to deal with it all herself. I wrote off this whole town because of him.

No wonder people hate me now that I'm finally back. They look at me and see my father. They see another runaway. Another person who abandoned them for something bigger without a backward glance.

I look up, surprised to find the fence has ended. I've circled all the way around to the front of the house without realizing, and now my feet, almost by habit, have led me away from the fence line. Toward the big tree out front, the one I first noticed when I pulled up. The one some part of me remembered, even when my conscious mind didn't want to.

The tire swing is still hanging from its thick lower branch. Up close, I can see that the rope doesn't look damaged at all. It's grimy, dirty from all these years out in the weather. But it's thick and steady as ever, and the tire dangling from it looks exactly the same way it did years ago when I took my last spin on it.

I can see it now. Me and Grant. He still scrawny, but starting to get taller, leaner. Starting to have that athletic build that would eventually turn into every muscle a guy can possibly have.

Back then, we'd play tag across this front field, barefoot. Chasing a couple of the neighbor kids, having them turn around and chase me in return whenever I managed to catch one of them.

Grant would always grin when he caught me, apologize through that gap in his front teeth, a gap that's long since vanished now.

I remember the way I used to catch him

stealing peeks at me whenever we'd sit down around the dining room table in the kitchen for lunch. Mama would be out back eating with the grown-ups, his parents, and other kids' parents. They'd leave us to our own devices, and we'd shoot eyes at one another, elbow each other for taking the last slice of bread, eating the last helping of stew.

I remember later on. When we were older, maybe at the start of high school. Just before he made friends with the jocks. Before that group of kids all drifted apart, before we made other friends, forgot about each other. I remember him pushing me on the tire swing out front, the way I'd scream higher, then shriek with fear, delight, some mix of it all.

I remember the two of us standing opposite one another on that same tire swing. Pushing it around and around until the rope was wound up tight. Then standing up at the same time, letting go, so it spun as fast as it could. We'd hang onto that rope, our hands touching, both of us shrieking. But our eyes were locked the whole time, like we couldn't get enough of that feeling. That adrenaline rush, and… each other.

I used to wonder if he wanted to kiss me. I used to think about it. I even almost kissed him, once. But Mama came out, called me home, and I let the moment pass.

I let Grant Werther go.

My feet lead me across the yard, until I find myself standing below the tree. I circle the tire swing, taking it in. I tug on it once to test its weight, and I'm surprised to find that Grant's right. It is sturdy. Maybe even as sturdy now as the day my father first strung it up.

That's why I never think about this. About any of it. It hurts too much to think about anything right after Dad's leaving. But it's been here all along, at the back of my mind, tugging at my subconscious.

My memories of Grant are all tangled up with Dad leaving, with heartache and pain. But still,

I never forgot him. Still, I knew him again the moment I saw him. I'm still the girl I used to be— *and he's still the boy he was too.* My brain was trying to remind me, trying to show me what I so desperately wanted to forget.

I walk past the tire swing, letting it drift back and forth on its rope as I approach the tree trunk instead.

Sure enough, I find it on the first try. The set of initials carved one on top of the other. Almost like the initials kids would carve later, in high school, with their sweethearts. We hadn't dared to put a heart around it back then. Neither of us wanted to admit we liked each other. That would be putting ourselves at risk, going too far out on a limb. We just circled it, flirted, made eyes at one another the way kids do, without ever taking it farther.

But I remember. I remember lying on the grass out here with him late one night, before sophomore year of high school started, before he made it onto varsity track and drifted away, started hanging out with the athletes, the hot girls, the cool kids. Before I lost him—before I pushed him away so far that he couldn't help but let himself get lost.

I wanted to kiss him. I wanted more. I never had the nerve.

I reach out and brush the tree trunk.

SB

GW

Right there in front of me. The evidence I'd been looking for all along. Grant and I used to be close.

But he abandoned me first. He started hanging with another crowd, stopped coming over to the farm. *He never kissed me.* That's the part that really rankles. He never took this chance when he had it.

Then I came back, gave him another chance all over again, and he got angry.

Angry because he thought I forgot him. He believed the same thing I did. I thought he forgot, he thought I forgot…

No wonder he's pissed, I realize. It's the same reason I was so angry at first.

Suddenly, it all makes sense. A little too much sense, and it makes my skin itch, to know that I've hurt him, too.

I trace my fingers across those initials, over and over.

Deep down, I'd always believed Dad was right about this town. *This place is a waste,* I remember him shouting at Mama, late at night after they both thought I was in bed. The year before he left. The year he traveled all the time, tried not to come home at all if he could help it. The year he spent trying to talk Mama into leaving with him. But she wouldn't budge.

This is my home, she said. *I like this life.*

I can't stand it, he'd always say. *How can you live like this, cooped up? Trapped? There's a whole world out there. Opportunities! We could make so much more money doing the same thing we do in a bigger city, out in the Midwest...*

I believed him. Deep down, even though he's the one that threw us out, ran away... I always believed he was right. I left here as soon as I could, went chasing my dreams. Success, money, my big-shot career. That was what life was about. That was what was important.

No one would ever abandon me again, as long as I had those things.

But that hasn't proven true. Guys have dumped me, and I've dumped guys, over and over. I've never really connected with anyone I've dated, not long-term, not enough to trust them to stick around.

And my money, my career? What has that brought me? A whole lot of anxiety about getting more. More money, a better career, the next promotion, and then the next and the next and the next. I'm never satisfied with what I have. I always want more, but more doesn't satiate me either.

Maybe less is what I really want. Maybe less

is actually more, in the grand scheme of things…

I turn away from the tree to squint back at the house. The farm house where Mama grew up, and her parents before her. The farm that's been in our family since as far back as Mama knew to tell me about.

There's a light on in the living room. I can't make out anything more, but I figure Grant must be inside somewhere. Showering or sleeping, if he's angry enough.

I take a deep breath of the fresh air. Hope that it clears my head enough to say what I want to say without stammering, losing my place, getting distracted.

I cross the lawn and quietly turn the handle on the front door. Step into the living room. He's not there, but the kitchen light is on too. I follow that to find him still in his work clothes, chopping vegetables on the counter, his shoulders taut with tension. There's already something bubbling on the stove beside him. Dinner, probably, or lunch for tomorrow. He always cooks when he's upset.

Strange that I know that already. Strange how fast I've gotten to know him. But then again, maybe not strange at all, given how well we knew each other before. It was only a couple of summers that we hung out, but it was long enough. I'm the same girl, and he's the same guy.

I step up beside him.

"Hey."

He keeps chopping the vegetables, quiet, unresponsive. But he's listening, at least.

"I thought you forgot me," I say. "I believed the same thing you did."

He turns to look at me then, but his dark eyes are unreadable. Inscrutable in this low light. When he finally speaks, his voice is low. Full of pain. "How could I possibly forget you, Sasha?"

I press my lips together, a tight line. "You abandoned me first, Grant. You started hanging out with the jocks, stopped coming by the farm. Never asked me to any of the school dances, never kissed me, when there were so many chances, late at night out watching the stars…"

"I wanted to kiss you every single one of those times," he finishes, eyes still locked on mine. Then he sighs and tears them away, shoulders still tense. "I didn't have the guts. I thought you weren't interested, anyway—you were hanging out with the artsy crowd, never asked me over—"

"Because I assumed you were busy being a cool kid," I point out.

"And I thought you were too important for me. I thought you left me behind, the way you left everyone here behind when you left town."

I bite my lip. "I never meant to do that to you. I just needed to get out of here. After Dad left, after everything Mama went through… I couldn't spend my whole life here. I needed to get out. Try something different. See what the rest of the world was like."

"And what do you think?" He lifts a brow.

I dare a tiny half-smile. "The rest of the

268

world? It's overrated, if you ask me."

For a long moment, he keeps chopping veggies. Dumps them into the pot, then slowly sets down the knife and turns to look at me. This time, I can read the pain in his gaze all too well. "I'm not a kid anymore, Sasha. I'm not going to beat around the bush. If you're just looking for a vacation fling before you head back to the big city and your life there, that's fine, but you'd best tell me now." He meets my eye, and I cannot look away. Can't tear my gaze from his. "What do you want, Sasha?" he asks.

I blink, startled. It's a question I haven't been asked in a very long time. It's a question I haven't asked myself in even longer. I haven't dared. Because if I were being honest, I'd admit that I don't want the life I currently have. Everything I've built for myself, my little empire in the city… It's everything I always dreamed of. Everything I thought I wanted. And it makes me feel nothing except stress. Sadness. Emptiness.

He sighs, deep in the back of his throat, and starts to turn away when the silence stretches on too long. But I grab his arm, pull him back to me, and blurt the only answer that comes to mind. The truth. The one that came into my head the moment he asked the question, even though it seems crazy.

"I want you," I say.

He steps closer. Looms over me. My head tilts back to keep our eyes locked, and my heart beats in my throat at his nearness, the scent of him, the feel of the heat radiating off his skin. "Are you sure about that?"

"As sure as I've ever been of anything," I whisper, and it's the truest thing I've ever said.

Grant cups my cheek gently. Leans down to kiss me, and this time, when we kiss, it's different. I sink into him, falling up, as I wrap my arms around his neck to steady myself. It's a slow, sensual kiss, the kind I could lose myself in for hours. His mouth parts, his tongue traces my lips, slides between them, and I tangle my tongue in his, lose myself in him, his taste, his scent.

We part again, and he hovers inches from my lips, his breath hot across my cheeks. "If you stay with me... If you want a life with me... You know that means living here, don't you?"

"I do," I murmur.

His eyes search mine. "Can you really accept that, Sasha?"

I open my mouth, but he stops me with a tilt of his head, a flicker of his brow.

"Don't answer this lightly," he admonishes. "I know how eager you were to run last time. How badly the big city tugged at you. You couldn't wait to put all of us—this whole town and me, in your rearview mirror. Are you sure you could really make a life here? Would you really be happy in this town?"

I lean up to press my lips to his, tentative at first, then deeper, harder. When we pull apart again, I know. I wrap one hand around his neck and tug him down until his forehead rests against mine, our eyes fixed on one another. "I want this, Grant. That life, the big city, all the hustle and bustle, it… I enjoyed it, for a time. But it never felt real. It never felt settled. This, *you*… This feels more real than any of that ever did."

"What do you want to do about the farm?" he asks softly.

I bite my lip and shake my head once, hard. "I don't want to sell it. I can't imagine it, not after everything we've built here, not after fixing it all up like this… Together. We built this place. My family built this place, way back when. I want to keep it." Then I wince and step back a pace to watch him. "But, I mean… I know I only own half the place now. If you want to sell, I can respect that. I'll…" I shake my head. "I don't know. I'll figure out another place to live…"

"I don't want to sell, Sasha," he cuts across me. "I never did. Hell, when you told me you did…" He grimaces, and it makes my heart ache to see that pain on his face. "It felt like a slap in the face," he finally murmurs. "You finally came home, and all you wanted to do was get rid of everything left that might tie you even a little bit to this place. That, and you acted like you didn't even remember me."

"Yeah, well, you pretended you didn't know me either." I cup his face between my hands, his beard scratchy against my palms. "I don't know how either of us ever believed that of one another, Grant. I'm sorry for that. But I remember you. I remember it all. I always have. Not just the bad parts, the only parts I let myself think about for years. I remember how much I loved it here, before Dad left. Before I started to worry that everyone would leave me, eventually…"

"I won't," he promises, and I smile, as I lean up to kiss him again.

"I know," I whisper against his lips, and it feels like a new start. Then Grant grabs my hand, tugs me away from the sink, into the living room.

We don't even make it as far as the

bedroom. We fall in a tangle of limbs onto the couch, both of us tearing at one another's clothing.

I don't know how I couldn't see this sooner. How I could ever run away from this place—from a man like Grant–when he's the first person who's ever made me recognize how miserable I really was in the rat race of the big city. Here, I've seen the stars every night, tasted fresh air, worked up a sweat at hard physical labor that I never dreamed I'd be capable of doing. But I'm stronger than I thought, and capable of so much more than I ever dreamed.

Just look at how quickly we shaped up this farm. In just under a week, we've been able to make it look like a completely different place, a real home, and a farm that could start working again. Imagine how much we could do if we lived here full-time, really put our all into getting this place up and running and producing again?

I love this place… And, I'm starting to realize, as Grant kisses me until my lips ache and lowers me down onto the couch, lying atop me, his muscles hard against mine, his body hot and close... *I love him.*

Grant tosses the last scrap of my clothing aside just as I finish pushing his boxers down, freeing his cock, already rock hard at attention between us.

But when he sits back down on the couch, he grabs me and pulls me onto his lap, until I'm kneeling across him, our lips still pressed together, tongues entwined. He pulls me down slowly, angling me just right, and then I lower myself the rest of the way, pushing the tip of his cock between my lips into my entrance, and slowly, inch by inch, lowering myself onto his thick shaft. I moan, head falling back as I sit down against him completely, and he fills me up, stretching me the way he always does.

Fuck. I will never get tired of this feeling.

"I love your tight little pussy," he murmurs against my lips, and I grin into our kiss, nipping at his lower lip. He bites mine in response, hard enough to make me gasp, and then he kisses it better, his hands tightening on my ass, lifting me up.

"You feel so fucking good inside me," I whisper into his mouth, as I slide back down against him, thrust him in deep again. We start to rock in time with one another, building up momentum, and with every crash of our hips together, the tension in my pussy builds, my clit throbbing with desire before long. His hipbone grinds against my clit every time I sit down against him, and it makes me wild. His hands run down my back, nails raking over my skin, as I cling to him so hard I'll leave marks on his back for days. I don't care. I want everyone to know.

He's mine.

And I'm his. And fuck, it feels good.

When he comes, it sets me over the edge too, both of us crying out, his hands pulling me down against him, his cock deep inside me as he finishes. I sag against him, spent, and he holds me up, supports me as I catch my breath, my heart hammering in my chest, my limbs limp with pleasure.

Before I've even completely recovered, Grant scoops me up in his arms. Carries me out of the living room, toward the bathroom, with a grin.

"I think we'd better get cleaned up before bed," he says, though to judge by the wicked smile on his face, I have a feeling we'll be getting dirtier again before we get cleaner...

Chapter 12

Grant Werther

I never imagined it could feel this good to be with someone. But then, of course, it is because it's *her*. The one who got away. The one I spent those summers years ago chasing after, and more summers than I care to admit after that—after we drifted apart, after we went our separate ways, she with the hip crowd and me with the sporty one—reminiscing about her. Wishing I hadn't let us drift apart. Wishing I'd had the guts to make a move when we still talked.

After she left, I gave up. Moved on. But I never forgot about her. The first girl to set me on fire.

Now, out of nowhere, she's back. Back, and mine at last. And I'll be damned if I let anyone tear her away from me again.

We're standing together in the old-fashioned

bath of the farm house, the shower steaming hot against our skin. I can't stop touching her. I lather up my hands with soap, mostly for the excuse, and playfully pin her against the wall as I run my palms down her sides, around to cup her firm, tight ass. Then I drop to my knees in front of her and trace my hands down each of her legs, one after the other, savoring the smooth feeling of her skin under my hands.

"You are so fucking sexy," I tell her, gazing up at her across the flat plane of her belly, my mouth inches from her tight pussy. The pussy I just finished fucking so hard that her thighs and her mound are still a little red from the force of it.

Sasha grins down at me and runs her hands through my hair, her nails scratching against my scalp, a sensation that sends a pulse all throughout my body, straight down to my cock, where I'm already starting to get hard again just looking at her, touching her.

"You might have mentioned that," she tells

me, a playful little smirk on her lips.

"Well, once clearly wasn't enough." I tilt forward to kiss her hip bone, then the side of her stomach, then across her abs, moving closer and closer to her navel even as I murmur against her skin. "I don't think I'll ever be able to tell you just how fucking gorgeous you are. How I can't get enough of you." I flick my tongue into her navel and grin as she shivers against me, forceful enough that I can feel it. I run both hands around the backs of her thighs and grip her tightly, pull her against me. "You make me insatiable, Sasha Bluebell."

"Only fair," she whispers as her hands tighten in my hair, and her body tenses, her shoulders leaning back against the wall to brace herself. "Since you drive me wild, Grant Werther."

"Only fair," I agree, my smirk widening as I trail my tongue from her navel down toward her shaved mound. She gasps and twists a little when I reach the top of her mound, and I can tell she's still sensitive from earlier. I'll have to go easy.

But that's fine by me. I like taking my time with her. I savor every minute I can get with this woman.

Gently, I pry her legs wider and trace my tongue across her mound. When I reach the crease where her upper thigh meets her hips, I trail my tongue up and down that, waiting until she moans faintly before I shift over to the other side to do the same there. When her hips start to buck against the wall, I bring my hands back to her ass, cupping her tightly, just hard enough to pull her forward a little, make her lean against me, as I duck my head lower to taste her sweet pussy.

I lick along her outer walls first, slow and careful. But she doesn't tense, doesn't seem to have any pain. If she's sore, it's the good kind of sore, so my slow, gentle licks don't cause any discomfort. Before long, Sasha's moaning my name faintly, and when I steal a glance up at her, like I've been doing all along because I love this fucking view of this woman, she's got her eyes closed and her head back, lost in the sensation.

I part her pussy lips with my tongue and lap slowly along her slit from back to front. *Fucking hell*. She tastes amazing, as always. An addictive, almost sweet flavor that I cannot get enough of.

"Don't stop," she murmurs, her breath coming faster now. She doesn't need to tell me twice.

With a faint growl at the back of my throat, I pin her against the wall, the hot water from the shower still cascading down our shoulders and over our skin, mingling on my lips with her scent and flavor. I lick her faster, my tongue toying along her slit, driving her wild. When she's bucking against me, and her hands fist so tight in my hair that it makes my eyes water, I push my tongue deeper between her lips. Find the entrance of her pussy and press my tongue inside, as deep as I can.

She cries out faintly, a soft sound that makes my cock throb with lust to hear it. It makes me want to take her again, right here. But not yet. Not until I make her come for me, over and over.

I love the sounds she makes when she comes, the way her pussy tightens, the way her eyes go unfocused and hazy. I love everything about giving her pleasure, and I want to give her as much of that as I can, for as long as I can.

I start to rock back and forth, thrusting my tongue in and out of her pussy, fucking her with my tongue, making it as thick and flat as I can so she feels each push. I'm rewarded with the sight of her belly muscles clenching, the sound of her soft moans. I curl my tongue inside her and drag it down her front inner wall, right across the little nub of her G-spot, and she cries out, still sensitive from earlier. When I clamp my mouth completely over her pussy, my lips touching her clit while I continue to fuck her with my tongue, her knees quiver.

"Fuck, Grant..." But she can't manage more than that, because I'm already pulling back a little, flicking my tongue up her pussy and across her clit. "I can't..." Her legs are going even shakier just from my ministrations, so without waiting for her response, I lean back and wrap my hands around her hips. I pull her down beside me easily, then lean her back against the bathtub, pausing to kiss her once, deeply, my tongue in her mouth, so she can taste herself on me.

"I'm not done with you yet," I promise in a low, certain voice, and I love the way her eyes light up at that, every bit as hungry for me as I am for her.

I slide down the tub, leaving Sasha directly in the warm rush of the shower, lying with her head back on the edge of the tub as I lift her hips to my mouth and start to lick and suck her clit in alternation.

"Right there, fuck, Grant, right…" Sasha reaches for my head again, grips my hair tight and pulls my mouth hard against her pussy. I love that— how hungry she is for me, how much she loves feeling me eat her out.

"I'm gonna come," she gasps, and that only

makes me lick her harder, faster, right over the sensitive spot that I know will set her off.

"Fuck, fuck…" Her words dissolve into faint, wordless cries as she hits her peak. But I don't stop there. I keep going, lapping at her clit and her lips, alternating between pushing my tongue inside her and swirling it around the hard little nub of her clit until she screams again, her hips bucking.

I lean up and slowly, gently, press my fingertip against her pussy entrance. Work it into her, an inch at a time, all the while watching her face, loving the way she's flushed with pleasure, her eyes half-closed and glistening with desire.

"Did you like that, naughty girl?" I ask, grinning. I push my finger another inch into her to accentuate the point. Her pussy muscles tighten around me, her mouth parting with want. "You like it when I make you come so hard you scream?" I press my finger the rest of the way into her, twist it gently back and forth so she can feel me in there, stretching her, pulling at her walls. "You like having my finger in your pussy."

Her eyes lock on mine, though it takes her a moment to catch her breath. "Not... as much... as I like... your cock inside me," she manages, starting to smile a sly little grin of her own.

I'm already rock hard again by this point, but I smirk at her, because I love making her impatient for me. Even as much as I want to be inside her, fucking her again, I want to draw this out more.

"Being impatient again, City Girl."

She bucks a little beneath me. In response, I curl my finger and run it along her inner wall, back and forth, right over the spot I know will set her on fire. She gasps, and I laugh softly, enjoying the sight.

"City girls like... things fast," she replies, trying to shrug.

"Here in the country, you'll have to get used to a slower pace," I reply as I add a second finger and slowly press it against her entrance. "We like to

286

enjoy ourselves. Take our time." I push my second finger into her, and savor her faint gasp, the tightening sensation of her pussy around my thick digits. "We know how to enjoy ourselves."

"I'll say," she breathes. I lean down to kiss her chest, up to her neck, my fingers still buried in her pussy. When I reach her mouth, she grabs me instead and kisses me hard, her tongue slipping between my lips into my mouth, tangling with mine.

I finger her until she comes again, her mouth pressed against mine so I can swallow her gasping cries whole, savor every inch of her body shivering under me and her pussy clenching around my fingers.

Only then do I sit back and pull her upright. The water's gone lukewarm beside us, but neither of us cares. I pin her against the wall and lift one leg around my waist, wrap it there tight as I press my cock against her pussy, rubbing it back and forth along her slit to coat myself in her juices.

"Tell me what you want," I whisper against

her mouth, and she smiles, the edges of her lips digging into mine.

"I want you to make love to me, Grant Werther," she whispers, and I swear to God, in that moment, I'm gone.

"Anything you want, it's yours," I murmur back. I raise her leg a little higher and slowly press the head of my cock into her entrance. Feel her swell and stretch to accommodate me, and with every inch farther into her that I press, I feel more and more complete. When I'm fully buried inside her, we both pause, our breathing coming hard and fast, our hearts hammering as we stand there, drenched in the shower, in *our* shower, in the house we share now. I have never felt this complete, this fulfilled.

Sasha bucks against me, impatient as ever, and with a grin, I lift her off the ground entirely and wrap her legs around my waist, her shoulders back against the tile wall. I fuck her until we're both lost in it, so distracted we don't even notice the water go cold around us. I'm lost in the feeling of her tight pussy clenching hard around my thick cock, the delicious sensation of being in her, possessing her to the fullest. She's mine, and I cannot get enough of her.

When I come inside her, I clench her hard against me, my voice hoarse as I groan with pleasure, feeling my cum shoot deep inside her pussy. I fucking love that feeling, the feeling of my seed coating her walls, claiming her, marking her as mine. And I love how much she loves it, her head falling back as she cries out.

When I finally pull out of her, I grin at the hot rush that trickles down her legs, joining the cool water swirling around our ankles in the bathtub now.

"I think we need another shower," I say, lifting an eyebrow, and she bursts into laughter as I wrap my arms around her waist and pull her into another long, slow kiss.

"I'm fine with that," she murmurs, arching

her hips to press against mine. "Though I think a cold shower is the only way either of us is going to cool off tonight."

She can say that again, I think, as I reach past her for the soap, to start getting clean all over again. If we can manage it this time…

Chapter 13

Sasha Bluebell

Ten Months Later

"Hey Hank!" I wave across the street to Hank, posted out front of his store with his legs kicked up on an ottoman and a newspaper spread across his lap. Must be a slow day for hardware sales. I can see Etna through the shop window, standing at the counter bent over a paper of her own. Probably doing the crosswords like she loves so much.

"How's it going?" Hank calls back with a pleasant smile and a wave. "You get that tractor working okay?"

"Grant's on it," I call back. "Thanks again for ordering the parts for us."

"Anytime." He winks and settles deeper in his chair as I walk past, on a mission to finish my shopping before Grant gets home from his own errands. I want to start dinner before he has a chance—I have a big special meal prepared tonight, but knowing my man, if he beats me to the kitchen, he'll show me up by starting some fancy grilling of his own.

Not that I'd complain, of course. But tonight I want to treat him, dammit. It's probably the last time I'll be able to for a long while, after all.

"Sasha!"

But of course, in order to finish my grocery store run, I'll have to be able to make it through town without everyone and their mother stopping me along the way to chat. Still, when I see who it is, I can't help grinning back and stopping to let Meredith catch me up.

"How'd your soiree go?" I ask with a grin when she reaches me.

Meredith heaves out a sigh, clutching her side, since she just jogged a few blocks from the communal parking lot to catch me. "Decent. Wish you guys had been there though." She shakes her head with another sigh. "I love the Johnsons, don't get me wrong, and Troy's a hoot. But nobody quite gets my sense of humor like you do. And poor Joe was bored out of his mind without Grant there to distract him with a few rounds of darts."

I laugh. "Believe me, Grant was sad to miss it too. Next time, I promise," I swear, but Meredith only raises an eyebrow and glances pointedly downward.

"You sure about that? Because you look about ready to burst, honey."

I laugh again and follow her gaze, one hand resting on my round stomach. "Still got another month in me," I reply. "I can make at least one more of your monthly parties before I'll be bedridden."

"Bedridden, and then sleep deprived from the constant fussing of your brand new baby," Meredith points out helpfully.

I roll my eyes. "You don't have to rub it in."

"I'm not rubbing it in! I'm only

commiserating. Since, you know…" She pauses, then her cheeks flush.

My eyebrows shoot sky-high. "Meredith?"

Her eyes widen and she clamps a hand over her mouth. "Crap. I wasn't supposed to tell. Not till the big announcement…"

"Oh my God. You guys are expecting?" I'd jump up and down with excitement if my big belly could handle it. But at eight months pregnant, I know better than to try that. So I settle for grabbing her upper arms and squeezing with excitement. "That's so wonderful, congratulations!"

"We'll have to set up some play dates for them," Meredith gushes, beaming. "They'll be so close in age, they can grow up together." She lifts her eyebrows and glances at my belly pointedly. "Who knows? Maybe you'll have a little boy and I'll have a little girl…"

I burst out laughing once more. "And they can play around on our tire swings together and fall madly in love?" I lift an eyebrow, my gaze drifting up the street into a brief daydream. "Well. Worked out for me. Who knows?"

She grins and squeezes my shoulder, and I smile, watching the little sleepy town for a moment. I can't believe that once upon a time I hated it here. Hated it so much I ran the first chance I got. I can't believe everyone else here was so mad at me, too. I'd thought they were all judgmental, mean-spirited, mad at me for leaving. But really, they were just upset that I ran away without ever looking back or saying goodbye.

Now, they've welcomed me back with open arms. Now, as I look up the street, I catch at least three of my neighbors glancing back, waving, smiling cheerfully, some on their way to Hank's shop to buy more supplies for their own houses and farms, others on their way to the grocery, same as me.

Meredith links arms with me and we stroll up the street to finish my errands. Once, this small-town life seemed impossibly boring to me. Too basic, too slow. Now, I adore the pace here. The way I can take my time, amble along and catch up with all my friends on my way to prep for the dinner I'm going to cook for the love of my life.

Now, I couldn't imagine spending my life anywhere else.

My stomach sinks a little as I pull up to the farm, car filled with the supplies for tonight's big dinner, and I spot Grant's truck already parked in front of mine. Damn. I hope he's not doing his usual thing, beating me to the punch on lovely surprises.

But when I hop out and unload the car, I find the house and the kitchen empty. That's good, at least. But if he's not making dinner yet, and if we've already finished the field-work for the day, then where has he gone?

I wander out back to scout the fields. From the back porch, a big, broad porch we added on to the house early in spring, I can see all the way across the main fields. We've planted almost all of them, except the couple we're saving for our late summer crops. I was worried when we got started about how we'd keep this all up, but we've been able to hire a couple of extra hands to help out around here, a super sweet couple who live a couple farms over.

Not only that, but we've already made headway selling some of our earliest crops to local farmer's markets and produce shops. It turns out that all my experience in the big corporate world of New York has translated into a pretty savvy marketing head back here on the farm. I've been putting in extra time branding everything we make —organic, home-grown, fresh from the land, just like the two of us.

Our company name helps too. *Country Meets City.* For some reason, that's clicked with a lot of people in the towns around us. Guess there are more city runaways who've come to roost back home than we thought.

We aren't making huge amounts of money, but it's already enough to keep us afloat, and Grant thinks that within the next couple of years, we'll be turning enough of a profit that we can expand the house a little bit. Add an extra bedroom for our little surprise in the oven.

We don't know yet whether it's a boy or a girl. We're waiting to be surprised on delivery day. But we already know that either way, no matter who our baby turns out to be, they're going to have a beautiful, perfect life out here in the countryside. We're going to make sure of it.

Smiling now, with the sight of our productive fields in my mind, I stroll out across the fresh grass, barefoot like always now. I've always hated shoes, but never so much as I do since this bun turned up in my oven. Now, when I have to run into town for errands, I can't wait to get home if only to kick off my shoes off and feel the grass between my toes, the solid dirt under my feet.

Just another thing I'd forgotten about before, back in my city life. Back when I forgot who I was, what I loved, what kept my heart beating and my mind alive with excitement.

It took Grant to remind me. To show me that everything I thought I had to run away to find was really waiting for me back here all along. Just like him. My man that got away—recaptured once and for all.

"Grant?" I call out, crossing around the house toward the front.

Then I spy him, and I pause in my tracks for a moment, watching.

He's up on a ladder in the tire swing tree. From the coil around his arm, I can see he's re-stringing the rope with a new one, one he must have picked up from Hank and Etna earlier today. He's bent over his work, busy, so I don't disturb him yet. I just slowly stroll closer, my eyes raking over his form as he works. I let my gaze linger on his strong biceps, his muscular back. He's got his shirt on, but

299

it's warm out here for an early summer evening, and that shirt sticks to his skin, shows off his muscles to perfection.

I drink in the sight as I meander closer, watching him work.

Only when I'm about five feet away does he finally hear my feet padding in the grass and glance back over his shoulder. His eyes catch mine, and my heart flips over in my chest, the same way it always does whenever we see each another. The same way it has since the moment I laid eyes on him out in front of this farm, almost a year ago when I pulled up this driveway. I'll never get sick of the way his eyes light up when they catch mine, like I'm everything he's ever dreamed of and more.

"Hey honey," he calls as he finishes tying off the rope. He runs his hand through his hair, pressing it back from his forehead, and my gaze drifts to his arms again, the bulge of his muscles, the delicate trace of his veins.

"Hey babe," I call back. "What are you up

to?" I squint at the rope and lift an eyebrow. "Decided this was unsafe after all?"

He laughs and starts to climb down the ladder, glancing from me to the swing and back again. "I still think it would've held our weight," he says. "But better safe than sorry." He reaches the ground and shrugs, giving the rope a solid tug. "I wanted to make this safe in time for our kid to enjoy it."

I glance from the rope to the tire at the bottom, then lean against the tree and cross my arms. "Well?" I ask.

He lifts his eyebrows. "Well what?"

"You going to finish?" I nod my chin toward the tire. "I think if you're trying to make this stable for our kid, then we'd better give it a go first." My smile widens. "You know. Just to be safe. And maybe for old time's sake."

He laughs softly. But he reaches down and scoops up the tire anyway, and starts to loop the end of the rope around it. "Anything you want," he replies with a wink. "It's yours."

I wait until he's finished tying off the swing to approach. He offers me a hand, and helps me up onto the tire. I grip the rope tightly, then he wraps one hand around mine, extra pressure to hold me there, and steps onto the opposite side of the tire. The branch doesn't even creak, even when Grant bounces a little to test our weight.

"Seems sturdy to me," he says, eyes locked on mine. "But we haven't done the full test…" Without another warning, he reaches down to kick us off the ground into a slight swing. I squeal, though of course with his hand around mine, holding me to the rope, there's no danger in me falling off.

We swing gently back and forth, eyes locked on one another, and I chill runs through my body at how familiar this is.

"I still can't believe you thought I forgot you," I whisper, my voice low faux anger.

Grant laughs and rolls his eyes. "I can't

302

believe you thought *I* forgot *you*." He reaches out with his free hand to cup my jaw. Gently draws me toward him and into a soft, slow kiss. "But hey," he whispers against my mouth. "All that really matters is that we've finally both remembered, right?"

I smile and lean my forehead against his, our eyes still locked. "Believe me, Grant Werther. I'll remember everything about you until the day I die."

Chapter 14

Grant Werther

One Month Later

I grip Sasha's hand—or rather, allow her to grip mine, so tight that my fingers scream with protest. But I can't complain. Really, really can't. It's nothing compared to what she's feeling. "*Fucking hell*," she screams—or at least, I think that's more or less the gist of it. It's hard to tell, since she's out of breath, and the morphine has made her a little bit loopy.

"Deep breaths," I urge her, rubbing her back, smoothing her damp hair back from her forehead.

"One last push," the doctor calls from the end of the table. It takes every ounce of self-restraint I have not to leap up from my seat, run down there with him to see. But I promised Sasha I'd hold her hand, stay with her. And no matter what, I always keep my promises to Sasha.

"Come on, honey," I coax, and she turns a glare on me that could probably set half this room on fire.

But she does it, screams and tightens every muscle in her body, giving one last huge effort. Then I hear a sound that breaks and makes my heart all at once. A sound that changes my life forever. Both our lives.

All our lives.

I hear a high-pitched, wailing cry, and the nurses on either side of the doctor start clapping, even as he reaches up to cut the umbilical cord, starts wrapping the little bundle in his arms up in a towel.

I watch, my heart swelling, aching, so painfully full that I worry I'll burst right here.

"It's a girl," the doctor says, and I turn to catch Sasha's huge, amazing, gorgeous, sexy, beautiful as hell smile, a matching idiotic one spreading across my face too.

The doctor lays the baby in Sasha's arms, and I kneel at her side, watching our little bundle of joy open tiny, baby blue eyes and coo at her mother. When those eyes meet mine, I know right in this moment I would lay down my life in a heartbeat for this baby girl. For Sasha.

For my family.

I've never felt so whole as I do in this moment.

"She's beautiful," I breathe. Sasha turns to face me then, and I have to catch my breath, stop myself from pulling her against me and kissing her until we're both out of breath. "You're beautiful," I add, and she laughs and groans and leans back against the bed, eyes back on our beautiful baby once more, our little miracle.

"Bullshit," Sasha says, her voice soft and weak. "I just pushed out a damn baby, I'm not beautiful right now." She laughs.

But I cup her chin gently and turn her to face me once more, shaking my head hard. "Sasha," I say, my voice low and serious. "You have never been more gorgeous than you are in this moment, right now."

She swallows hard. Smiles, a little half-smile, my favorite kind. The secret ones she saves just for me. Then she lifts her arms, and my gaze drops to the other most gorgeous woman in the room.

"Do you want to hold her?" Sasha asks.

And my whole life begins, right now.

THE END

Author Biography

Penny Wylder writes just that-- wild romances. Happily Ever Afters are always better when they're a little dirty, so if you're looking for a page turner that will make you feel naughty in all the right places, jump right in and leave your panties at the door!

Other Books by Penny Wylder

Filthy Boss

Her Dad's Friend

Rockstars F#*k Harder

The Virgin Intern

Her Dirty Professor

The Pool Boy

Get Me Off

Caught Together

Selling Out to the Billionaire

The Billionaire's Gamble

Seven Days With Her Boss

Virgin in the Middle

The Virgin Promise

First and Last

Tease

Spread

Bang

Second Chance Stepbrother

Dirty Promise

Sext

Quickie

Bed Shaker

Deep in You

The Billionaire's Toy

Buying the Bride

Dating My Friend's Daughter

81177194R00176

Made in the USA
Lexington, KY
12 February 2018